THE BLACK COOK'S HISTORIAN

THE BLACK COOK'S HISTORIAN

Graeme Rigby

Constable · London

First published in Great Britain 1993
by Constable and Company Limited
3, The Lanchesters, 162 Fulham Palace Road
London W6 9ER
Copyright © 1993 Graeme Rigby
The right of Graeme Rigby to be
identified as the author of this work
has been asserted by him in accordance
with the Copyright, Designs and Patents Act 1988
ISBN 0 09 471630 7
Set in Linotron 11pt Pilgrim by
Rowland Phototypesetting Limited
Bury St Edmunds, Suffolk
Printed in Great Britain by
St Edmundsbury Press Limited
Bury St Edmunds, Suffolk

A CIP catalogue record for this book
is available from the British Library

for Ros

Acknowledgements

The traditional singer Benny Graham introduced me to 'The Black Cook', a nineteenth-century comic ballad. In a cunning display of sheer bravado, the hero cheats sufficient money out of a body-snatching doctor for an evening's drinking with his fellow sailors. The Black Cook in this book takes only his title from that song. There was a fashion in the seventeenth and eighteenth centuries for naming domestic slaves after famous generals. Scipio Africanus appeared in my head and was irresistible.

The poet Fred D'Aguiar read an early draft, offering both encouragement and useful criticism. A couple of months later he found himself in Bristol on a Guyanese Writers' Tour. Taking the opportunity to visit Henbury churchyard, where he'd heard there were some African graves, he saw the white marble gravestone of one 'Scipio Africanus Negro Servant to y Right Honourable Charles William, Earl of Suffolk and Bradon who died y 21 December 1720 aged 18 years'.

I'd like to thank Fred for his help and the others who also read and commented on the manuscript: Julia Darling, Barrie Ormsby, Rick Taylor, Abdulrazak Gurnah, Nigel Rigby, Mike and Janet Turner and my wife Ros. I would like to thank Simon Tepper for providing a literal translation of Juvenal, which I abused shamelessly. In particular, I would like to thank Northern Arts, who gave me a bursary to work on the novel, on the basis of a few, very early pages.

7

ONE

It's burning. I can see the flames here where there aren't any. Not rough hovels on the slopes of a hill, but broad white avenues as they were drawn in my imagination. They are burning and above these gracious mansions, the ship that was a palace; the palace that was a ship lifted out of an ocean, sailing on the waves of fire and on fire itself, masts, rigging and furled sails and the flags made of flowers, reds, oranges, yellows, blues and all the shades of purple, twisted into the ropes and lost in the flames that have taken on their colours, shrivelling these originals to black cinders and ash in the strong wind that fans a heat I still feel on my face.

I was born in A—, in the County of B—. By my best calculations, the year was 17—. It could have been the year before. If History gives us nothing else, it gives us latitude.

The County of B— isn't blessed with hills. As a boy I'd climb into the upper branches of any tree and see for miles. If the vast flat landscape felt like mine, it wasn't. A man can see further than he owns, which is just as well for those of us who have nothing, but it is the cause of all wars and destructions, nevertheless.

I never knew my mother. I only gradually became aware

that the lack was unnatural. The question of my origin I resolved privately in the possibilities of my father's arse, or of his belly button. He was not a religious man. It was Mary, the pig-keeper's daughter, who told me the story of Creation. In my imagination, I saw my father fashion me out of my unknown mother's rib. He was a butcher and handy with a knife. Even now, when I am old enough to know better and worse, I can imagine it. I see the mother I never saw, hanging from the rafters of the smoking shed. I see the deft flicks of the knife. It's an action of the wrist.

Doubts began to creep in as I inspected the hindquarters of a recently slaughtered sow and Mary offered to show me hers for a penny. Every bit of meat fetches its own price, my father used to say. I beat her down to a farthing as long as I didn't touch. We settled on a halfpenny. The pan collected the last drops of Fat Agatha, who was past breeding anything but puddings, sausages and cuts for the salt barrel, and I began to explore those things that remain hidden, when you look at the world from the top of a tree.

After I had satisfied my curiosity, we lay for a while, thinking about things. Looking up at the rafters, I saw my mother in an entirely different light, but it was too late to make any difference. We could hear my father singing his song, as he worked:

'Who is that jolly butcher boy?
    His name it is John Bone.
Pray, why does a jolly butcher boy
Live by himself alone?
    Well, why shouldn't he?
    Oh, why shouldn't he?
    He don't need a wife
    If he's quick with a knife
    And all the ladies have gone
    Fa la! Fa la!

10

Fa titty fa la!
Pray where have the ladies all gone?'

'He looks at me,' said Mary. Her words came out of
nowhere in particular. They were the first she'd spoken
since we'd settled on the price.

Her words had penetrated my thoughts one by one. It
took a while to connect them. 'Who does?'

'Your father.'

'Oh,' I said, looking carefully at her myself.

'Is it true what they say about him chopping up your
mother into pie meat and selling her cooked in her own
jelly and everybody said they was the finest pies they'd ever
eaten but they didn't quite taste like pork only you couldn't
quite pin it down and all the bones was ground down and
fed to the geese and they wouldn't let no one near them
that year on account of how they grew so fierce except they
were nice as nice with your dad even though he walked
with the shining knife in his hand and that horrible glint
in his eye and the only reason everybody still buys his pies
is they're secretly hoping he's going to marry again because
they was so delicious and it wasn't so much the meat
although that did taste wonderful but the jelly was so deli-
cate and juicy there's half a dozen as have offered him their
own wives at very reasonable knockdown prices?'

'Who says that?' I asked, allowing her words to roll
around inside my head for a little while before answering.

'Everybody. Well, Margaret Hooper says it and her father
goes to church regular and he's probably going to Heaven.'

'I never knew her.'

'Who?'

'My mother. I can't remember any pies that tasted like
anything but pies, but if I can't remember her I probably
wouldn't remember the pies because she wouldn't keep for
more than a few days unless he salted her down and then

11

he wouldn't get the jelly like that.' My father didn't say much to me, but he had taught me the trade.

'Well, he frightens me,' said Mary. 'He looks at me funny with his eyes. Doesn't he frighten you, Will?'

I thought about the question for a moment. 'Yes,' I said. 'I'm always frightened of him. Aren't you frightened of your father?'

'Oh yes,' she said. 'He looks at me funny as well.'

'Do I look at you funny?'

'You look at me like you're falling out of a tree and you can't make up your mind whether to shut your eyes or keep them open, but it's all right because I'll catch you and I'm soft to land on, well, I've got soft bits anyway, softer than you and they're getting pillowy, are you going to ask me to marry you?'

'What would you say if I did?' I would get my halfpenny back, I supposed, or maybe she would buy some sweets and we could share them and I'd get at least a farthing's worth, maybe more if I ate quickly.

'I'd say maybe, maybe not, William Bone. Are you going to Heaven?'

'I don't know,' I said. 'I hope so.'

'You probably aren't, because you weren't supposed to look at me in that place until we got married and I don't know if I'm going to marry you if you aren't going to Heaven. Dick Hooper's going to Heaven. All of the Hoopers are and Margaret says I might be too and if I married you maybe I'd go to Heaven and you wouldn't.'

I recognized the force of her argument. I longed to be back in the trees.

'You could always say sorry. That might make it better and then I'd be able to marry you. You could give me another halfpenny and I could give that to God, maybe, and then everything would be all right and we could live happily ever after.'

12

'I'm sorry,' I said. 'I haven't got another halfpenny.'

She took the news, theologically, in her stride. 'Well, maybe I could have look at yours and that would be fair because it would make things even and God wouldn't mind.'

'What about the halfpenny?'

'God won't mind that. He'll see it as a token of your love and you'd have to give me one of those if we are going to get married.'

I have always gone along with the superior understanding of others. The strange feelings she awakened could have been love, I supposed; were love, I was sure, so sure that I cried out, 'Marry me!' all of a sudden, surprising her and she laughed out loud and my father burst through the door and she ran out, no longer laughing but burning bright scarlet and I will always remember it.

My father beat me soundly but said nothing at all. He looked at me. Perhaps he had always seen me strangely, strange was his normal. He fingered his knife, but I could not penetrate his thoughts. Perhaps he feared a breach with the pig-keeper. Perhaps he could see Mary dangling from the rafters. I tried to imagine the grey smears of ribs she had shown me, split from the breastbone. I tried to imagine her in neatly butchered joints; to count her in pies, spread out on the counter for the eager eyes of the whole village, crowding forward for just a taste of her delicious jelly and my father smiling a mysterious smile, but he wasn't smiling. His face was a concentration of cunning and despair. He had put broth into my bowl and I ate it, spoon by spoon, every mouthful, in silence.

If I never came close to understanding my father in the years that led up to these events, I never saw him again after. I never again saw the pig-keeper or the Hoopers, who may or may not have gone to Heaven by now, individually or all in the one go, with or without Mary, whose face, grey pale or bright scarlet, I never saw again either. I was never again in the county of B—, although in all the years following I could not climb a tree or a tall mast without it coming to mind. All of it. My father's eyes became the eyes of God, following me through half a dozen dreams in which he told me I would not, on any account, be going to Heaven. It did not seem inappropriate to see God serving in a butcher's shop, smiling at the customers and telling me that I was going to Hell as soon as he could be bothered to lift me down from the hook.

'What delicious pies,' said the customers.

'I only use the best cuts,' said God in my dream, whose eyes were pools of cunning and despair. 'The secret is in the jelly.'

TWO

I woke up aware of fire. The heat of it was against my face. There were flames and a black face peered into mine. It was very black and the eyes were very red. Even with my scant knowledge of religion, I recognized a devil when I saw one and I screamed heartily.

He hit me over the head with his great ladle and I lost consciousness again, my dreams filled with stars and fire and the certainty of damnation.

With a degree of caution, I found myself looking into the same face and the same eyes. At the edge of vision, I was aware of the same ladle. 'I'm sorry,' I said, although the words did not quite break through the barrier of my lips, only managing to dribble incoherently down my chin. 'Am I in Hell?' I asked as he came into proper focus.

'You are,' he laughed. 'You are. So are we all. Ha!' And he laughed even louder.

'I'm sorry,' I said again.

'And so you should be, for I am a very black devil and you are my pot boy.' Behind his face I became aware of other faces and they were laughing too, only they weren't black faces, but ordinary faces with just an average degree of cruelty in them.

'He wants you, so he's got you,' said one of these faces. 'He's a very black devil indeed, but he's your master now,

15

boy, and you're his slave, because that's what a pot boy is so there's a turn-around for you and no mistake. The black bastard's got his own slave.' He laughed and his companions laughed and the black face laughed.

'What d'you make of that, then, Africa?' Another voice from another face.

'I have taken a liking to him,' said the black face, so close to mine that he blotted out every other detail in a total eclipse. 'He suits me, but I think he needs more sleep.' He raised the ladle and I passed out again, to the sound of rough laughter.

The sea is a prison. Prison on the other hand seems like a drifting ship with no sign of land. A passing whale might seem like a country. Hope flaps like a flying fish stranded on the deck. They are not much use as food.

No.

A prison is like a prison. A ship is like a ship. The sea is the sea and there is no hope in any of it. A flying fish, on the other hand, would provide a welcome variation on the diet.

I had been sold to a press-gang on a recruiting expedition inland. Sailors are at home in a flat landscape.

'Do you know what a press-gang is, boy?' I was on my own with the black face now, trying to focus in a way that would not give offence.

'Yes, sir.'

'You have been taken by one. Have you ever seen the sea before?'

'I think so.' He looked at me with a degree of uncertainty narrowed into his eyes. 'Sometimes on a clear day from the top of the great oak in winter when there aren't any leaves

16

to get in the way and you can see for miles, sir. Sometimes I think I have seen the sea. What does it look like?'

'You'll find out soon enough,' he grunted. I could see that he was just a man now, like the Son of Cain at the rarey show with the collar and leash and the raw meat hanging from his teeth, who roared at everybody, especially children, and he tried to catch the women but he always cowered in submission when his master cracked the whip, but I saw him eating an ordinary plate of bread and cheese when I crept out to where they were all sleeping on the outskirts of the village and he just smiled at me and offered me a piece of cheese. I ran away. This was not Hell, but ordinary cruelty. A form of logic would run through it somewhere. Sooner or later I would be able to trace it.

'Have you ever seen a black man before?' he asked, noting my interest in the shape and colour of his face, which I was trying to hide for fear that it would make him angry.

'Yes, sir. You were at the rarey show. You were the Son of Cain.'

'I have got many names,' he said, 'and none of them are my real one. I am called Scipio Africanus Major. It was a joke, but it suits me. Have you read Livy?'

'I can't read, sir,' I admitted, uneasily.

'I will teach you to read and write. You will hear me called Skippy the Nigger. They will shout for the Black Bastard. Africa, you old Black Bastard, they will say. I am the Black Cook. You will call me Mr Africanus, because you are to be my pot boy. What is your name?'

'William Bone, sir.'

'Good,' he said. He spoke quietly and slowly, measuring out each thought with precision. It was as if he were explaining things to the night. 'Far be it from me, a man with no acknowledged issue in this world, to comment upon parental responsibility. Your father sold you for a shilling.' He, himself, had never been a Son of Cain. That had been

17

someone else. There were many black people in the world. He came from the continent of Africa, which was full of black people. Everyone was black there, except for a few white people. He had been sold to these white people for a bag of sea shells. 'We have something in common, you see.' He was a freed man now, but freed did not mean freedom. 'The world is full of relative values, although it seems that your father does not place a very high value on his relatives.' He laughed at that thought for a good few minutes, laughing and repeating it until I realized that I, too, was supposed to laugh. I laughed and we laughed together for a few seconds and then he stopped.

If there was a name to the ordinary cruelty that became my new life, it was HMS C—. In truth, however, the navy was no more cruel than my father. If Mr Africanus was more cruel than my father, it was because he was more determined. My education was the unfortunate focus of his determination. If, in this account of my life, I appear to have an almost educated voice, unlike the one to be expected from the son of a village butcher from the county of B—, it is because this voice was given to me by Mr Africanus, the Black Cook.

He was, indeed, the very devil when it came to grammatical accuracy. Each of my questions was answered first with the ladle, second with a correction, thirdly with a reply.

Blow, for example.

'Ow! What of I did wrong?' (For example.)

Blow.

Correction: 'What wrong have I done.'

'Shit' (I rub my head). 'What . . . wrong have I . . . done?

'You have not applied sufficient energy in the cleansing of that pot.'

'What?'

Blow.

18

Correction: 'I beg your pardon, sir.'

'I beg your pardon, sir?'

'You have not applied sufficient energy' (and the Black Cook mimes a demonstration of scrubbing) 'to the cleansing of that pot.' (He brings my head to the pot.) 'Behold, William Bone, grease. Do you understand?'

'Yes, sir.'

'Good.'

These were the first steps in my education. First and foremost, I learnt not to ask unnecessary questions. I learnt to supply gaps with plausible fictions, adjustable according to need and without recourse to any higher authority. Truth, for example. It's a habit that has never left me. He was a good teacher. I did my best to learn what I could, but I was a late starter. Words still induce a sense of panic. Sometimes, I know, it forces me to finish my sentences too quickly, desperate to get rid of the responsibility they bring. Sometimes, I will start a sentence and it seems like a mountain I don't know why I'm climbing, but the top is just over the next rise, although it isn't and I don't know whether I should go back down again or carry on climbing and, although I am not normally scared of heights, here I become scared of heights and that is why I keep climbing, because looking down makes me even more scared, so I grasp at convenient projections on a rock face that is getting steeper by the minute, my feet are scrambling and all I am aware of is the fear of falling, because so much of the slope is falling away beneath me, like scree and then I am at the top, unable to remember whether I wanted to be here or not and the world is made up of ordered fields laid out before me which could be mine, except for the small cross, marking the very summit, which is a full stop and a reminder that this is someone else's kingdom.

Language was a kingdom for the Black Cook; the first part of this strange earth that he conquered. Even without him,

I navigate by means of the landmarks he has left for me. If I could see them more clearly, I would tell you a simpler story. You are ill-served by your narrator. In all fairness, I have to tell you this now.

The Black Cook, on the other hand, was cast in an heroic mould. In another time and another place, his story should have been told by historians of an appropriate stature. It was his misfortune, and mine, that he had to make do with a pot boy.

'Sing me a song,' he said, one day, as I scrubbed away at my duties.

'Who is that jolly butcher boy?' (I sang.)
   'His name it is John Bone.' (I answered.)
'Pray, why does a jolly butcher boy
Live by himself alone?
   Well, why shouldn't he?
   Oh, why shouldn't he?
   He do . . . does not need a wife,'

(I improvised quickly at some cost to the melody, adjusting the phrasing of the next line accordingly and trying to carry it off with bravado, my eyes focused on the ladle as he tapped out the momentarily confused rhythm.)

'If he . . . is quick with a knife
And all the ladies have gone.
   Fa la! Fa la!' (I smiled hopefully.)
'Fa titty fa la!
Pray where have the ladies all gone?'

'And did you learn that at your father's knee?' he asked.
'Yes, sir.'
'It has probably lost something in the handing down.'
'Yes, sir,' I agreed.

'Do you like music?' he asked.

I nodded vigorously, expressing the kind of enthusiasm that I hoped would find favour. He smiled and I smiled in the temporary good fortune of his smile. Between our smiles he introduced a violin.

'You will learn to play this. I like music.' He looked at me closely. 'We both like music, William, so you must learn to play it well.'

I assured him of my intention to please him in every respect and he patted me on the shoulder before turning back to his cooking. It was fortunate that his love of music found a different expression to that of his love for the English language. Violent blows were replaced by liberal encouragement. He would never hit me while I was playing on the fiddle. I practised at every opportunity and could soon hold a tune. I bought tuition with scraps from the galley, with rum when I could get it, approaching any sailor who had the least musical ability. The Black Cook smiled as I made up the small parcels of bribes. I did it in secret, knowing that he knew I was doing it and that he was happy in this small expression of initiative.

I think I have been in prison for a long time. It is a flat landscape with no vantage points and the days pass with very few changes. My fingernails still grow, but they say that fingernails continue to grow even when you are dead, like headless chickens running about, or perhaps more like rats leaving a sinking ship. I have come to know about rats. The hair also, I believe.

The least we should be able to expect from death is that it will be complete. What other bits will carry on without me? If there is no end in sight, are there any true beginnings and where should we look for a middle? And what is a story without a beginning, middle and end?

I have tried to discuss the matter, but rats are not interested in philosophy.

'In the beginning,' they say, 'there were teeth. Teeth made all things in Heaven and Earth, so they could come together. Give us a story we can get our teeth into,' they say.

'Where shall I start?' I ask them.

'Start anywhere you like,' they say. 'We do not care about structure, but if you do not give us stories, we shall eat the clothes off your back and then, when you are naked, we shall eat the flesh off your bones.'

'Shall I be dead?' I ask them.

'You will be unable to tell stories.'

I have been given paper and ink and pen, but my words will never reach the light of day. Some of the pages are chewed even before they are finished. I will not reach the light of day again, either. Or, if I reach the light of day, it will be only for the brief moments before an execution. There will be sunlight and swarming crowds. Ballads will be sold and these true confessions will be amongst them, a speculative printing at the publisher's expense: a quick killing in the market that will exist while my feet dangle in the air. They will be indistinguishable from all the other lies and forgotten before I am cut down and I will be buried, even though parts of me will still be alive, but it won't be like that.

THREE

I will tell you the Black Cook's Story: the story he told to me, not the larger story that I am telling you anyway. I will try to put it together in some form of order. It came to me in bits and pieces. Some he would repeat over and over again. Some he only mentioned once in all those years I knew him. And some elements I have supplied myself, to prevent the whole project collapsing on its uncertain foundations.

THE BLACK COOK'S STORY

Africa was too small a continent, though she did indeed stretch from the wave-lapped shores of sweet Maroc, east etc. to the steaming heat of the Nile, to the tribes of Ethiopia. Juvenal speaks thus of Hannibal, the great Carthaginian general who was defeated by my namesake. Yet, it was in Africa that I was born, in a kingdom that you have never heard of. It was a land of plenty.

My father had many slaves and they were treated well. I was part of a large family and I was loved, the third son of a favourite wife. As a child, I played in the dust and made empires in the mud of the riverbank. Safe within the walls of my village, I imagined the worlds I would conquer upstream and downstream and out beyond the farther bank. I would practise the throwing of the javelin

23

and I would engage in mock fights with my brothers. As I grew older, I would explore further. I would take my javelin and practise in the hunting of wild animals.

On one such expedition I was seized by strangers and two of my brothers were seized with me. With our mouths and our arms bound, we were made to march. I was about ten years old when this happened. Many miles and many days and many tears. I cried because I knew that I would never see my home again. I cried, but all the tears of the world will not make mud out of a dusty road. My brothers cried also. There were many others, men, women and children, who were forced along the same road. They cried as well. No one cried while they were marching, for we marched with our mouths bound, our captors not wanting this loud misery to alert passing villages to their danger. Gathered in a safe place, when the day's march was concluded, however, the gags were removed and the ropes were removed from our arms, although chains were fixed to our legs. Then we would eat and cry and sleep.

I had never seen the sea. I had never seen a white man. These twin calamities were now visited upon me. My tears had long subsided into the grief which has no voice left. I had never seen a sailing ship. It did not seem to belong to the same world as the canoes that paddled past my cities of mud. The white men paid for us with the shells that form the currency in those parts and we were herded into a cargo hold, manacled in wooden stalls and stacked one upon the other.

Sickness, hunger and impossible heat; the dying packed tight against the living; piss, shit and darkness. There were no more brothers. If my brothers were on that same ship, I did not see them any more. I only saw food and water and glimpses of light.

After many days, many weeks, I was sold in another

24

land and my owner was a Major James Tulliver, who wanted a little gift for his wife and family. The Major had his tailor run up a costume for a little Roman general. Ha! Ha! I turned about for the Major, who was pleased and who told the tailor that he was a capital fellow. On the voyage to England, the Major taught me the rudiments of the English language, with the endless patience of a man training a dog. I saw only food and water and glimpses of light and was a quick learner. I was placed in a large box, that was tied up with a bow and that is how I was presented to the family.

'He is our little Roman general,' said the Major. 'He is Scipio Africanus Major,' the Major announced to peals of laughter. It was a joke the Major had been planning for a long time.

'He shall have to study his Latin if he is a Scipio, Papa. He looks more like a Hannibal,' said the Major's pink son, a boy of about the same age as me.

'Oh, yes, Papa. He will have to attend his lessons.' The daughter clapped her hands in delight.

Her name was Lucy. Her brother's name was James, like the Major, his father, who now laughed and Mrs Tulliver laughed and the children laughed. I was Scipio Africanus applying myself to my education, careful never to shine too brightly. I was Master James' companion, a constant sparring partner who was always careful to end up on the ground. I would fetch things for Miss Lucy whenever she called: 'Oh, Scipio.' I would carve her little dolls out of pegs and she would say: 'Oh, Scipio, our little general,' until one day Mrs Tulliver decided that her daughter was becoming too old to play with generals, who were not little any more, and with Master James going away himself, Scipio Africanus was to be sold to an acquaintance of the Tullivers, who needed someone who could work in the kitchens, but could be dressed up in

25

a wig and a fine jacket for the occasional dinner party.

The name of Scipio Africanus stuck with me. It was a collar around my neck, but it was my collar. The servants would call me Africa. I would earn small amounts of money writing letters for them. I borrowed books from the master's library. No one noticed. It was a classical education. I read of soldiers and great empires; of great battles and men; of Scipio Africanus and Hannibal of Carthage. I learned how to cook. Little by little I saved, from my writing, from a hundred other schemes. I approached my owner and asked if I could buy my freedom. A price was set that was thought to be far beyond a slave's means. I had meant to set out into the free world with some small stake, but I parted with all of it. I was 'manumitted, emancipated, enfranchised and set free'. To compensate for the excessive price, I took a volume of Livy's History of Rome from the library and secreted it amongst my belongings. I was alone in the world and on the streets. I looked about at the paleness of the country and decided I would not find freedom there. If Africa was too small a continent, I would go to sea. I would cross oceans. I would see the world and find something to my liking. I signed on as a cook upon a ship of the line.

This, then, was his story. Sometimes he would tell it boomingly, the words filling his chest in the pride of his anger. Sometimes he would bark out small resentments as if each one were a knife. Sometimes he would say nothing at all but the argument was visible within him.

If I do not write flames on every page, it is not that I can't see them. The flames have caught hold. The time before that great burning and the time after it are both ablaze,

26

now. These words burn merrily and even the rats have coats of fire.

I served him on the *D—* and on the *E—*. I went with him on the *F—*. I was no longer his pot boy, but at the same time I was still in his service: within his protection. He educated me.

He collected people with the bait of food and rum and would hold court in his galley on an easy day, when the ship was becalmed. He constructed a protection for himself out of the debts he did not call in. He made the largest jokes and laughed the loudest of all, drawing his courtiers in and flashing his broad grin at them.

'Call me Africa. Empty my larder, boys. Have another cup of dark rum. I'm a dark continent, boys. Hold him steady while I pour it down his throat. Ha!'

His expansive generosity was measured out cup by cup and calculated with precision. Sometimes he would be punished for an unlicensed liberality, but the word could never describe his action. 'I've got a broad back,' he would say. 'The scars do not show so much on a black skin.' He would pick one out of any group and make him legless. The others, with the merest taste of it on their lips, would share in the spectacle, their tongues hanging out in anticipated pleasure. As the rum dribbled down the drunkard's chin, they would vie with each other to prevent any wastage, licking it off him in turn. When the poor man was completely lost, the Black Cook would lift him up off the floor and hand him over to his eager companions. 'Take him away. Do what you like with him. Roll him any way you want. He's had too much for his own good, boys. Ha!'

He would spend his own free time studying charts. If he could acquire books of foreign travels, he did. He would make detailed explorations of any port we came to, studying its fortifications, its palaces and citadels. Sometimes he would take me with him. Usually he would find a young girl down by the docks and pay her to keep me company while he went off. Sometimes he would return with another one on his arm; sometimes mine would have to do for the both of us.

It was in the port of G—. He had found me a mulatto. I spent the day with her, most of it asleep in a stinking cot, in a room filled with other stinking cots, other sailors and other women. I woke up feeling the sweat around my eyes. In the cot next to ours, a one-legged man was labouring over the black body of another girl. I watched his arse go up and down for a while, as he struggled to balance in his task on one knee and a stump. Through the flames I recognize that arse burning with zeal. I see you, Josiah Peabody, and I know you. If I knew then what I know now, I would have broken your back as you laboured there, but someone was being sick on the floor. He was laughing and vomiting and wiping his mouth across the face of a woman whose eyes were empty as she manoeuvred herself beneath him and searched his pockets. I wiped my own eyes and looked at the mulatto, who shrugged. I didn't know whether she was shrugging about the man being sick, or at the woman with her hands in his pockets, or the way I had fallen asleep on her. I smiled for a moment, not knowing quite why, but she caught the movement of my lips and smiled back, holding her fingers like a peg on her nose. I pulled her up and moved towards the door, lurching suddenly into the yellow light of a late afternoon and breathing in fresh air that was only a marginal improvement. She followed me. She had been paid well to look after my needs until the Black Cook returned and he hadn't.

We sat in the street with our backs against a wall. She tried to revive my interest for want of something better to occupy the time.

'He hasn't come back.'

'Is all right,' she said. 'Enough money.'

'He should have come back.'

'Tomorrow morning I kick you out.'

'We will find him.'

It took many hours, searching through the back streets and around the docks. The girl held my arm as we walked. She stood beside me in a hundred drinking shops as I asked if anyone had seen him. She made no response to the voices calling out:

'Can't handle her by yourself, boy?'

'I'll handle her.'

'Come here, girl. Don't want a boy when there's man's work to be done.'

'What d'you need a nigger for? Cock too small for the doxy?'

'How about this one, girl? Big enough I reckon.'

She made no complaint as we walked. We would stop and rest and then move on. I was becoming increasingly concerned. She showed no emotion. We went back to her cot to ask if he had shown up there, but he hadn't. We lay there for another hour. I would turn my head at every movement and she gave up trying to hold my attention. If she felt any exasperation, she never showed any. We went out again. We came back. We went out again. We came back again.

It was three o'clock in the morning. She had fallen asleep. I couldn't sleep and then, suddenly he was there in the doorway. I shook her awake. At first, he didn't speak. His forehead was an open wound and the blood was caked with dirt and splinters of wood and dust and it had dried into his hair and into his shirt and his eyes were burning through the blood with something that was more than anger, that was horror and resolve and rage. His hands were bound behind his back.

29

I cut through the rope with my knife and tore a rag from the girl's bedding. We went outside. She held a lantern, while I cleaned him up, spitting into the rag and wiping away the blood. He flinched when I tried to tend the wound on his forehead, but he said nothing. When I had finished, he stood up. Both the girl and I stood back, looking into his face and expecting words to come out of it, but they didn't. He turned on his heels and strode off. We followed, half walking, half running to keep up with him.

It was a shack of kinds, by the edge of the River H—, that reaches the ocean at G—. It was raised at the front on short poles. Attached to the back, where the wooden floor poles were driven into the slope, there was a lean-to. The splintered and broken slats lay on the ground. Its roof had caved in, the main support pulled through the wall and now lying useless.

'They took my papers.' They were the first words he had spoken. 'I believe they are in there somewhere. Would you fetch them for me?' He indicated the main shack and I took the lantern round to the front to investigate.

Inside, a number of people had fallen asleep where they had finished drinking themselves into a stupor. At first I trod carefully, but they were all too far gone to worry about. Nothing would wake them. The Black Cook had shown me his manumission papers often enough that I knew what I was looking for. I found them on a table, beneath someone's head.

'Fetch a price,' he slurred as I lifted him off them. He fell forwards again before he had finished speaking. I took the papers with me, glad to be out of the place.

Africanus and the girl stood with arms full of kindling that they had gathered nearby. Underneath the shack, there were already three good-sized piles. We spent another ten minutes gathering wood. There was a mesmeric quality in the Black Cook's anger and we worked in silence. He

30

appeared with the roof support from the lean-to and fixed it across the door, before climbing underneath the shack with the lantern.

The mulatto was brushing the dirt from her dress.

'You didn't see anything.'

'Is all right,' she said. 'He pay till morning, you do what you like. I kick you out and everything never was.'

We watched from a safe place while Africanus worked methodically at the lighting of each fire. He seemed oblivious to the possibility of someone passing by. Nobody did. He stood back and admired his work. When he was content that each fire was well alight, he turned and walked towards us. As we made our way back through the town, I turned several times to catch a glimpse of the blaze as it took hold. I imagined the faces lifted from the tables; the drunken screams; the inability to move. He didn't turn around once. After a while, he slipped his arm under the arm of the mulatto and smiled.

I slept in the street, with my back against the wall. I dreamt about flames and about Mary the pig-keeper's daughter. The great oak was on fire and she was crying, 'Jump!' and lying in her rough cot with her arms stretched out wide to catch me.

It was morning and the mulatto was pushing Africanus out into the street, as small as she was, as big as he was. He was laughing. He pulled me up and we made our way back towards the ship.

With an iron collar on his neck, they lead him through the streets of the city; the broad avenues of white-faced houses with their terraces decked in flowers; the palace above them as they go down, this ship that has been lifted out of the sea and carried across mountains; flames. No. The sun has lifted and it shines, now, through the masts and the rigging

31

and the flowers and the citizens, who, saying nothing, see nothing. The morning sun is in their eyes and he is invisible to them; has never been.

He rubbed at his left eye, that was inflamed. Stray fragments from the wall of his prison had worked their way beneath the lid and back. I tried to raise the subject one time, but he struck me a blow on the side of my head that sent me sprawling. The eye became worse. We were far out at sea and the salt air added irritation to irritation. It became swollen and the blood vessels burned.

He would allow no one to look at it, rubbing it constantly, wearing it down with his forearm.

'Let me look at it,' I would say.

'Destiny is a great elephant,' he said, 'crushing the things that are thrown in its path.'

'At least let me clean it. It's infected.'

He brushed my concern aside and talked about destiny, a constant subject with him.

THE BLACK COOK ON DESTINY

Imagine the span of a man's life as a line drawn between two points: from the one end, it is Destiny; from the other, we describe it as History.

Between Destiny and History, a man's life is continuous Suffering. If we have no sense of our own destiny, if we are not acknowledged by History, Suffering has no end.

Suffering, like Time, is measured from moment to moment. The experience of Time is the experience of Suffering. In all essentials, we are talking of the same thing, even though we might use two different words.

If we can grasp the line of Destiny, that is the line of

History, it becomes a staff that we can wield in our War with Time, which is the Conquest of Suffering.

If there are a thousand lives, there are a thousand staves.

The War with Time is the Conquest of Other People.

Nine hundred and ninety-nine staves must be broken.

It wasn't an argument. I offered no opposition. He let the words roll around his mouth before offering them up to the world. He savoured the taste of words. It was clear to me that my duty lay in remembering his wisdom. He would hold to a theme over weeks, sometimes. Having let it drop, he would come back after a gap of months, sometimes. All these sheets of paper are distillations of the fragments that remain.

I am writing a history for the rats, who will, with time, return all things to fragments.

He lost the use of his left eye.

'You watch but you don't see,' he said. (This was much later. It was another ship, I—, and a different ocean, J—. At his pots, he laughed and suddenly plunged the ladle deep into the mess of peas and salt pork. I wiped the scalding liquid from my face.)

'What am I supposed to see?'

'You are supposed to see what stands before your eyes.'

I looked.

'A simile is a comparison,' he said. 'By drawing attention to the similarity of two logically dissimilar objects, we cast a light on the subject of our gaze. He doth bestride the narrow world like a colossus, for example.'

33

He moved his legs and watched the tiny ships scurry between them.

'A metaphor, on the other hand, brings two incompatible elements together, so that there is a spontaneous combustion. It makes its own light, which burns fiercely from within.'

'Yes,' I said. Having fixed a definition, he would use it endlessly. These were popular with him. Through his remaining good eye, he consumed the world with an appetite. He saw words and searched constantly for the illumination in them.

'I am your subject.'

He stood like a subject.

'Mr Africanus . . .' I began.

'Continue.'

'Mr Africanus stirred the pots of History like an emperor in waiting.'

'Good, William.'

'I do my best,' I said.

'You see, you can be a quick learner,' he smiled.

'Yes,' I said, although the truth of it was, it had taken me five years to come to the realization.

FOUR

Let me describe my cell. The light comes from a small window about ten feet above my head, through which I can hear sea birds but rarely see them. Small birds sometimes fly through the bars and become confused. Beating against the corners of the cell, they sometimes fall back in exhaustion and settle on my table. Cocking their heads, they examine me with one eye, whilst watching the rats with the other. I sit on the floor, away from the light, pretending to be nothing. The rats, in another corner, make no moves either. I want the bird to find the window. The rats want the bird to come down to the floor. With opposing motives, we take the same action. If the bird does move down to the floor, I clap my hands and frighten it into the air again. The rats do not hide the bitterness they feel towards me on these occasions. They accuse me of cheating; of making up rules as I go along; of sentimentality and unreason. I am guilty of all these things. Experience has taught me that I cannot help the bird find the window. My movements have an effect on the movements of the bird, but it is random. Even within this confined space, the possible combinations of my movements stretch beyond number and I am tied to a series of horizontal planes stretching less than half the way up the wall, whereas the bird can utilize the full extent of the vertical plane. Its size and manoeuvrabilty allow it a lifetime of unrepeated combinations of single movements without ever once following the trajectory that would take it back through the window. Usually they manage to find their way out after a few minutes. When the panic subsides, they are aware of light and fly towards it. In my own case, I am still waiting for the panic to subside.

The walls are of rough, unfaced stone. Grey when the light falls on them. In the darkness, I lose control of colour. If I close my eyes, they can take on the blue of a remembered sky, or the deeper blues and greens of the ocean, or the yellow browns of the river, the colour of clay, or the rich greens of the forest. I touch the walls with my eyes closed, imagining myself to be sitting in a tree top and the air through which I can see for miles has become hard as glass, but it is not glass, it is a rough stone that has become transparent; or it is the world that has hardened, air, earth, sea, compressed to the texture of rock.

Sometimes, when I open my eyes, I am so close to the walls of the cell that I see they are not grey, even in the light. It is the light that is grey. The stones are made up of a thousand different colours that I don't have the names for. The light isn't grey either. On these days the walls sparkle for me. The light jumps between points on the surface of the stone, distances too small to measure, but forming a network of illumination as if it is alive with a kind of energy. I am trying not to say fire, but, yes, it is fire, although it is a different kind of fire. I touch it and see that my hand too is covered in light moving between the hairs, along the network of fine lines, the shape of which I can change at will, by flexing my fingers or clenching my fist. Light is trapped on the surface of the back of my hand, like the birds that become trapped in the horizontal and vertical planes of this cell, and it runs back and forth in the unrepeated combinations of direction, which represent infinity, and what I am, in fact, looking at in the stone is the skin of the stone and what I am looking at in the table is the skin of the table and if I look up at the small rectangle of the window, I see the skin of the rest of the world and that too has become a living thing, pulsing blue and orange and green and violet, words do not express the colours that I can see and when I look down on the rats, if they have come out of their holes between the stones, I see them through this blinding grid of coloured lines and shining with their own light too.

These are good days. On days like these, free from time and space I walk in a kind of eternity. There are other days, when it seems, merely, endless, and these are the bad days. It is fair to say that bad days predominate in my life.

I imagine Eternity as a vertical plane, whereas Time stretches out, ahead and behind, on the horizontal. For the sake of convenience, I have placed the present directly in front of me on my writing-table. When I get up and walk about, I move through Time. Sometimes I try a little jump.

I allot the periods of my life to the different paving slabs on the floor of the cell. They are broad slabs. There are one hundred and fifteen complete slabs and thirty-seven half-slabs. In addition, there are seventy-three separate rocks, bricks and broken fragments used to fill in the gaps. I shouldn't forget the eleven steps leading up to the door. I tell myself that I shouldn't forget the twenty-six letters of the alphabet, either, taught to me by the Black Cook so many years ago, in the combination of whose possibilities I have been bound ever since, as if the lines between them were made of string. I allot different incidents and different groups of characters to each slab or half-slab. To the separate rocks, bricks and broken fragments, I allot the people and incidents that have no meaning for me. I avoid them. I also avoid the eleven steps leading up to the door, which I am saving up for the end, if there is an end. If I could avoid the twenty-six letters of the alphabet, believe me, I would, but there are so many of them and there is only one of me.

For weeks, I will progress methodically through my life, careful not to step on the cracks. I never move anywhere in the cell, except through a strictly chronological progression. The path starts on the first paving slab beyond the table and continues in a route that has been designed to avoid crossing the same incident twice. It ends in the slab immediately behind my chair. When I lie down on my bench to sleep, Mary the pig-keeper's daughter is beneath my head, whereas my feet lie over G—. There is a hole in the corner of my cell for piss and shit. Out of propriety I make no allocation for this area. Perhaps I'm saving it up also. Every day I retrace my steps, having swung them round to stand on Mary the pig-keeper's daughter and Fat Agatha, until I am standing in the barely imagined territory of my birth. From then on, I move only forwards through my life until I reach the table, when I sit down to write. Sometimes, when I put down my pen, I start again, edging around the present until I stand on my beginnings. Sometimes, I retrace my steps, taking my life in reverse order, reflecting both on what I have written and what I have experienced.

It took me many attempts before the system had fixed itself in my mind and I was able to avoid an arbitrarily headlong rush of fifteen years in a simple step.

There are weeks, however, when the whole narrative progression of events ceases to have any meaning for me. I close my eyes and jump between incidents, blindly running the length and breadth of the cell and not knowing where I will end up and what connections I will make. I become quite dizzy. I laugh hysterically and roll about the floor like a pig rolls in his own muck.

I will spend weeks, again, where I wish that I had never

created this whole ghastly progression. It is a prison within a cell. It has become impossible to move any more, except in the terms of this narrative of my life, which I must write; which I need to write; which I am ordered to write; for which there is no purpose. There have been months, even years, when I have written nothing, but it doesn't make the time run faster or slower for me.

So I walk between the events of my life, talking to the rats, who will eye me curiously, or listen to me attentively, or ignore me completely, according to their mood and I will explain patiently, laugh wildly, or harangue them with vehemence, according to my mood. And it isn't even always like this. The time stretches out and I cannot count the numbers of my moods and the infinite combinations through which my moods swing, bouncing from wall to wall and never finding an exit.

Yes, sometimes, I shut it all out in despair or euphoria, neither of which are justified by any specific event, because there have been no events of any significance for so long, but that doesn't stop me, for the mind is a remarkable instrument. Nothing happens and yet I cannot move for incident, or, in the midst of these incidents that have become solid, I find myself able to move as if nothing has happened at all.

When I am writing, some days I do and some days I don't. I am given paper whenever I ask. Ink also. I write out a request on a sheet of paper and hand it to my gaoler. Fresh supplies come either the next day, or the day after, or a week later, sometimes even as much as a month or more. A clean sheet of paper can stare at me from my table for three weeks. Three days of a bare table and I am tearing strips from previous sheets and frantically making notes of the things that I must not forget and then the new paper comes and I throw them away, happy to forget anything I can.

I say my gaoler, but there have been more than one and I don't know if there are other prisoners in this place, to whom they also belong. He opens the door and I climb the steps in silence. If I am in one of my methodical moods, I hurry backwards or forwards through this history, aware of his silent impatience. I am handed a meal, a bowl of thin soup, bread, cheese sometimes. This happens twice a day. I don't complain. We don't speak to each other. He doesn't speak to me, because he has orders not to speak to me. I don't speak to him, because he will not speak to me. I have counted seventeen and none of them have said a word and I only ever spoke to the first one, until I had learnt that he was never going to reply.

The rats talk to me. If the rats didn't talk to me, I would probably go mad.

Rats do not give each other names, because they recognize each other by smell and, knowing each other with such clarity, have no need of abstraction. The rat whose smell is unrecognized is a stranger to be driven off. If the stranger isn't driven off, for whatever reason, his smell becomes familiar.

At first, I had a strong horror of them. They told me they were used to this. They didn't speak to me, at first, but when they started to speak to me, they explained those early days.

'Mankind doesn't like us,' they said. 'Nobody likes us, really.'

'Fleas like us,' suggested one.

'No,' said another. 'Fleas exploit us.'

'That's right,' several voices called out.

'Fleas are bastards,' came a cry from the back.

When I first came into my cell, there was a stick standing against the wall. My gaoler wasn't without mercy. When I saw the rats, I knew that the stick was there for killing rats. In those early days, I would wait at their holes with my

40

stick raised. I would lie on my bench with my hand clasped around my stick, suddenly leaping among them and striking out with fury.

I killed a lot of rats in those early days. I became quite accomplished. If the rats didn't talk to me in those days, they can hardly be blamed.

Rats, however, do not bear grudges. They do not mention those days, except in passing. Killings, for them, are in the natural order of things. They are social animals, but their idea of society is different to ours. A rat is either one of their number or a stranger until he or she is dead, at which point they become meat. It's a perfectly satisfactory arrangement. They have a similarly simple system of classi-fication for the rest of the animal kingdom: if you are smaller than a rat or weaker than a rat, you are food; if you are larger than a rat or stronger than a rat, you are to be avoided. Cultivating my friendship is a way of avoiding me, in their philosophical system.

One day, I simply grew tired of killing them. However many I killed, the number visiting my cell did not decrease. When I stopped killing them, the numbers did not increase. The volume of rats increases in proportion to their calculation of available food. When I started to offer them scraps of food, in addition to that which they took without asking, the numbers increased. When I withdrew the food, the numbers eventually reduced to their former level.

My study of rats took place over a long period of silence. They didn't start speaking to me until I withdrew food from them for the third time.

'Make your mind up.' I wasn't surprised to hear this voice after so long. My cell was ablaze with light, that day, and I was walking through Paradise.

'If the snake spoke in Paradise,' I thought, 'why not rats, here and now?'

41

'Is this some kind of game?' he asked. 'Are we supposed to be learning something here?'

'I'm walking in the eternal life,' I said.

'Only meat is eternal,' he said.

FIVE

The Black Cook collected people. Half-Done Dan, he collected in K—. Having left our ship in L—, we had made
our way overland to K—. I was beaten up four times on the
journey. Travelling with the Black Cook separated me from
my countrymen.

'D'you like blackies, then?' for example.

'We sailed together,' I might explain.

'Don't like sailors,' one of them might say.

'Don't like blackie sailors, specially,' his friend might
add, face lurching in towards my own, which would be
attempting a retreat.

'We don't like you, either,' would finish the conversation.

My bones ached and I was glad when we reached the
port of K—, where peculiarities are common and I could
walk unmolested. And yet, remembering those streets, I
see the one-legged Josiah Peabody, surrounded by his
congregation of saints, molesting me out of the corner of
his eye. He was not there, but he is there now, half a
leg and almost half the way through the alphabet. What
is it about K— that draws these one-legged men to its
beery embrace, Half-Done Dan with his right leg gone
and Josiah Peabody with his left, locked in eternal opposition? He is not there. Here in this cell, people spread
like fire. History oozes like the damp.

Half-Done Dan was a philosopher, and this was his philosophy:

HALF-DONE DAN'S PHILOSOPHY

I A ship is a nation in a bottle.

II A captain is like an extra bollock.

III 'You don't need captains,' says the man who wants to be captain.

IV The sailor who's no use at sea is abandoned on a desolate shore.

V It's no different anywhere else.

VI Show me the shore that isn't desolate.

He played the fiddle and would illustrate the variations on his philosophical system with a hornpipe of his own composition, called *God Help The Bollocky Sailor*. The Black Cook bought him drinks and listened.

If there was a thing he didn't know about the sea, he didn't know it. You couldn't teach him anything of ships and sails, either. He was the finest fiddle in K—. They'd taken off the bottom of his leg and left him with a fiddle as his only crutch in the world, but he'd fend off all comers.

He gave a hard look at my own fiddle, but I wasn't about to mount a challenge.

'Is this a desolate shore, then?' asked the Black Cook.

'I get by,' he shrugged with what he assumed to be a casual air.

'How would you like to be rescued?'

'It would depend on who was doing the rescuing.'

'Would you care for another?' smiled the Black Cook, giving me money and motioning me towards the attention of the innkeeper.

She was called *The Pride Of M—*, a converted collier, squat and shallow-draughted.

'She was built for black cargoes and that's what we fill 'er with,' laughed the Master, looking at Scipio Africanus with a twinkle in his eye. Normally, the Black Cook would avoid the slave ships. Here, we were searching one out.

'I am a good cook, sir. Maybe the best you'll come across, sir. And this one, here, sir, he's, oh, he's an experienced sailor, sir, oh yes, I can vouch for him, sir. Five years in the Royal Navy. Show him your back, Will. Hardly a mark on it. Do you see that, sir, and five years in ships of the line? Oh, he's a good man. And this one'll cost you nothing but his food. He helps me in the galley, sir. I'll look after him, no trouble. I'm a freed man, yes. Earned it from a grateful owner, whose life I saved. He was set upon by savages, sir, but I fought them off, though I lost my eye to a heathen arrow. I'm loyal, sir. Yes, sir. I've got my papers of manu-mission. All I ask is you respect that, sir, and you've got the finest cook you'll ever meet, whether it's for the economics of a long voyage, or for serving up a nice dish to the Master's cabin.'

'Well now, Blackie, if it's not all you're cracking it up to be, it's just a short drop into the hold, ain't it?'

'You won't be disappointed.'

'We'd better not be, Blackie whatever-your-name-is.'

'They call me Africa, sir. I answer to Africa.'

'Were there any rats on this ship?' I am asked.

Yes, there were many rats.

'We have heard tell of rats who were great sailors.'

You get rats on all ships. And when a ship is sinking, the rats are always the first to leave, scrambling down the sides of the stricken vessel and swimming out, away, all of them in the open sea.

45

'Rats are better sailors than swimmers.'

Most of them drown.

'All of them, most likely.'

I tell them the story of a shipwreck. I am alone, floating on a glassy ocean, a raft of broken planks between life and death from exhaustion. The sun beats down mercilessly. Is there a God in Heaven and has he forgotten me? It is a week since I have tasted water or eaten food. Surely, this is the end. The end cannot come too soon, between the merciless sun and the cold nights and the sharks that circle me. But wait! Is that a ship on the horizon? She's seen me. I'm hauled on board, an hour away from certain death, no more. I collapse on the deck, scarcely able to smile my thanks and as I lie there, a rat climbs out of my pocket and scurries away behind an old tarpaulin, before anyone can stop it.

'Did he really? All that time, he'd been in your pocket? Just sitting there quiet as quiet? Oh, we're bloody marvels.'

This way, I bargain for their attention. There was no shipwreck and no raft and no rat. They know it's not true and I know it's not true, but they would like it to be true and I also would like it to be true, because it serves its purpose and, now that I've said it, it is true, but I put it on a spare half-brick. It exists between us, but I won't mention it again. I won't step on it again, except by accident. The rats know better than to probe too deeply into such a story. The disillusion would spread into the rest of my tale and we'd be lost.

They like to hear about the sea, though, because they think they have an affinity with navigation. Apart from the sea, they like to know the practical details of any killings or love interest. They brighten up perceptibly, when there is the hint of such possibilities. In their ideal story, the Captain's mate would be his mistress, who had dressed up as a sailor to be close to him. On the wild, rolling sea, they

46

would enjoy nights of unfettered passion, before they were discovered and abandoned by a crew, who were both fiercely moral and jealous at the same time, on an island populated by cannibals. The Captain would be accepted by the tribe, only after he had eaten his lover. Or, perhaps, the lover would be accepted by the tribe, only after she had eaten the Captain. Or maybe they would eat bits of each other and the one that lived the longest would be accepted, or possibly finished off.

They would like that story.

I am saving it up for them.

The voyage to N— was bearable. The Black Cook cooked and he ingratiated himself with the crew and the Captain and the representatives of the Company. Old Jack Tarpit. Greasy Gravy. Darkie Deadeye. The crew vied with each other to come up with the best name for him. He laughed. For the most part, they just called him Africa, and as we drew close to the coast of it, this gave rise to a new string of jokes.

'Africa, you're a stinking black arsehole, intcha? Oh, sorry! No offence! I was talking to the country. What a stinking black arsehole . . . of a place . . . Africa. Ha! Ha!'

Or alternatively:

'How come Old Blackie got to be so brown? 'Cause he was born in a bucket of shit, that's why! Ha! Ha! 'Cause Africa is just a steaming hot bucket of shit. Ha! Ha! Ha!'

The Black Cook laughed.

'I am cut off from Africa, William,' he explained with a smile, 'in the same way that you are now cut off from England and Half-Done Dan is cut off below the right knee.'

I discussed the new and genial Scipio Africanus with Dan, but he had never seen the old one in his anger, although he sensed enough to show respect, himself.

47

'There's a purpose in it,' I said.

'That may be so,' Dan replied without commitment.

'You and I, we're part of his purpose,' I told him.

'Not me,' said Dan. 'If there was ever a purpose in me, it lived in my right foot, 'fore it went and got gangrene. Maybe it was purpose as poisoned it. There's beginnings and endings, William. I'll have no more to do with purposes.'

In the port of O—, we filled our hold. Roped together, they were brought out in small boats, staring at us and at the sea as if they were trying to take it all in. The Black Cook watched them and noted each one. The representatives of the Company counted them aboard, checking each against their manifests and satisfying themselves that there was no dishonesty. The sailors would slap the slaves on the back, comforting them with encouraging words.

'Nothing to worry about, Blackie. You come with us over the sea. You're a big strong lad. You'll be all right. Why, she's got a nice pair of titties, hasn't she? You'll do all right.'

Nets had been strung up along the sides of the ship to prevent anyone throwing themselves into the sea. Most of them seemed to be lost to the possibilities of escape, but there was no point in taking risks.

'Here's a nice one, Africa. You could make some little black babies with this one. Save up your money and you could do a little deal with the Company.'

'I'll ask them. Maybe I could have something on account.'

'Oh, they don't like used goods, Africa. Don't like them to be given a dose till they're over there and sold.'

'I'm clean as a whistle.'

'Bassoon,' the sailor laughed. 'Clean as a bassoon.'

The woman in question moved without understanding as she was turned about for the benefit of Old Africa. The sailor weighed her breasts in his hands, demonstrating the fullness of them.

'I could be tempted to a bit myself. Black or white, long as they've got the right bits, I say.'

The woman spoke several words in her own language, addressing herself to Africanus.

'What's she saying, then, Africa?'

'It's another language.'

'Well, I know that.'

'I'm afraid I don't.'

She jabbered on for a while, but the Black Cook turned away and she fell silent. The sailor pushed her along and down the ladder into the hold.

A slave ship's no easy life. There's the constant moaning and the clearing out of the dead and the stink. Sometimes there's silence, which is almost as bad. It would be enough, just to have to put up with the heat, but mix it with the smell of incontinent close confinement and a kind of sickness permeates the whole ship.

Sometimes we would have them up on the deck so we could wash them down with buckets of sea water. The hold was sluiced out, but you couldn't get rid of that smell. One of them managed to throw himself overboard. He couldn't swim and we gathered at the side of the ship to watch him drowning, but the yawl was lowered and a couple of sailors rowed over to him and hauled him out. He was still coughing out the water when they flogged him to death. The slaves watched in silence. He was tumbled back into the sea and they were pushed back into the hold. We were becalmed and the stifling heat had made everyone irritable.

Dan and I stood at the side, looking down at the reflection of the sky in the glassy surface of the ocean, broken, as it was, by the body of the dead slave.

'D'you know why they call me Half-Done Dan?' he asked into the stillness of the air.

'You lost your right leg.'

'That's where you're wrong,' he said.

I said nothing and he said nothing more and eventually I broke the silence.

'Why do they call you Half-Done Dan, then?'

'If I was to lose the other a-one, I'd be completely,' he said.

'Completely what?' I asked.

'Done,' he said.

I laughed, but he wasn't laughing. He stared down, seriously, at the water and he didn't look up. I stopped laughing and said nothing. I considered the various things that I could say, but none of them seemed to offer much comfort. It was ten minutes before he spoke again and in all that time, his eyes hadn't left the body of the slave as it floated away from us.

'If you was to jump overboard, you could swim back home in that direction.' He pointed vaguely towards the horizon.

'I wouldn't get there,' I said, not knowing where my home was, anyway, but he ignored me.

'If Africa was to strike out that a-way, he'd be swimming back and a-drowning in the direction of where he come from.'

'So?' I asked.

'I'd go round and round in circles. Like water down a drain.'

'What's the difference?'

'Hope,' he said.

I took the dead body as a starting point and imagined the inward curve of Half-Done Dan's path through the water.

'Your wooden leg would keep you afloat,' I offered.

'The wrong way up.'

He laughed now, but it foundered on the ocean of his

50

philosophy, sinking in his throat and not knowing whether to go clockwise or anticlockwise. These were the Doldrums.

'Was it the Cat?'
Was what the cat? The rats have caught me dreaming and I am suddenly confused.
'Did they flog him with the Cat O' Nine Tails?'
Who? I ask, my eyes still full of that glassy sea.
'The slave.'
'We know about the Cat,' a voice cuts in.
'I saw one only yesterday,' says another.
'What?'
'A cat. Bold as brass, like he owned the place and he was a big bugger.'
'We're not talking about cats.'
'I wasn't listening.'
'*The* Cat, we're talking about. *The* Cat O' Nine Tails.'
'What's that?'
'Somebody bite him.'
'Well, pardon me.'
'How many did they give him?'
Yes, I say.
'What?'
It was the Cat.
'Bold as brass.'
'How many did they give him, then? How many strokes?'
A hundred. They gave him one hundred strokes with the Cat O' Nine Tails.
'And was there blood?'
His back was raw meat.
'Lovely.'
He was dead before they reached seventy-five, but they carried on. No more screams. No more water from his lungs.

51

No movement from him at all, just the lash making his body jerk and the blood trickling from his back on to the deck, reflecting the sun.

'Lovely. We've heard tell of the Cat, but we never tire of it, do we? No, we don't.'

'A great big ginger tom. You never saw the like of it. The size of a dog.'

'Where?'

SIX

'In my dream,' said the Black Cook, putting down the precious volume of Livy and lying back in his hammock:

THE BLACK COOK'S DREAM

A man came to me and he wore my father's face. I have forgotten my father's face, but it seemed to me that this man was my father. He bade me follow him; keep my eyes fixed firmly upon him: he had been sent by his fathers and there was a purpose. He would lead me to a new land.

I was afraid, but I followed, looking neither to the right, nor to the left and it seemed that we were walking upon the surface of the ocean, a thing that was not possible. I was curious as to how this could be. What were the forces that supported me? I tried to keep my eyes fixed upon him, but curiosity became too strong and, at last, I looked down. All I could see was the surface of the water and a shadow that seemed to fall across my feet.

I looked behind and it was a vast snake moving across the sea. Its jaws were open so wide that the sun was almost eclipsed and the shadow rose across my back and I felt cold. Although no one had told me, I knew that the name of this reptile was Africa.

'What does it mean?' I cried out and the man, who seemed to be my father, turned to face me. He was angry.

'Who are you?' he asked. I said that my name was Scipio Africanus. He said: 'It means that you must keep your eyes fixed upon me and go forward.'

I put one foot in front of another and kept walking. I was walking faster and faster, trying to keep my eyes fixed upon him, but he was disappearing and I couldn't see him any more. I was trying to follow his instructions, but I no longer knew in which direction forward lay.

I keep walking and I can feel the water lapping around my ankles and I can feel the cold on my back, but I cannot bring myself to look down.

'That is how my dream ends,' he said.

'We're only a few days out of P—.' I couldn't think of anything else to say.

'They must leave the city,' he said, 'with no more than a suit of clothes. They must be unarmed. They must carry with them the memory of their wives and children.'

I left him.

My son, black as his mother, and my daughter as black as hers, as if I never had the strength to make a difference and I certainly don't now, but I still think about them. I would have taught them how to climb trees. There were so many trees and I would have taught them how to climb and find safety, looking across a flat landscape to the far horizons, except the land wasn't flat, but in my mind, climbing trees with them, it was flat and we could see for miles and they could see the village where I was born and the history of my life laid out between that village and the tree we now sat in, far up in the branches, right at the top, we're a hundred feet up and they can see everything and we don't speak, but we smile at each other, my daughter, Elizabeth, who is black as black and my son, Henry, who is only a few shades lighter, because I have told them everything I know, which is not enough to make a ha'p'orth of difference.

He came to us and dragged us roughly into the corner of the galley.

'There was a dog, once.' He spat the words in a hoarse whisper. 'The favourite of his master. Do you understand? The master wanted him fit for the chase, so he did not feed him. The dog did not understand, do you understand? He was hungry. He scavenged about until he came across some meat that had been left for the rats. It had been laced with poison, do you understand?' He cast his good eye over his shoulder to check that we were alone. 'He was a good dog. He was his master's favourite, but he ate the poison that had been put out for rats and he died like a rat. Do you understand?'

We nodded, even though we didn't understand.

'No food for William and Dan, tonight. Do you understand?'

'Yes,' I said, because I did understand, now.

'Good,' he said. 'Well, we'll say no more about it, then.'

A dog can choose to eat poison. To be a rat with other rats and die like a rat. Rats, themselves, wouldn't understand this. A rat would say: 'Save me or don't save me.' I was aware of hunger. Dan and I didn't speak. I could have saved them. Half-Done Dan could have saved them. Neither of us saved them and although we looked at each other, we couldn't speak to each other.

I walked and talked with the doomed men.

'Two more days, we'll be rid of the bastards. Wash the bloody stench of them out of her and get drunk. God, I hate 'em.'

Dan played a few tunes, but his heart wasn't in it. They wanted reels and jigs and hornpipes. One of them did a step dance, clumsily. I watched his feet, so I didn't have to look into his face.

They ate.

Not everyone eats at the same time, on a ship, but it was a slow poison. The officers and the representatives of the Company ate and the crew who weren't on watch ate and then, those who were on watch at the time the rest of the crew had eaten, ate too and everybody had eaten by the time it began to act on the first ones who had eaten and most of them were asleep, anyway.

It was in their stomachs. Some woke from their sleep, screaming with pain, helpless to do anything but realize they were dying. The cramps that seized them would not release them, except on the other side of the grave.

A panic set in. Those who were awake, or were woken by the screams of others, suddenly felt their own cramps. They shook each other and shouted at each other, searching for an explanation of this sudden plague. They read the fear in my face and in Dan's face and they thought it was their own fear of death. One of them put his arms round me and held me tight in the final throes of his dying.

The Black Cook ran from the galley holding his cleaver in one hand and clutching his stomach with the other.

'Ahhhhhh!' he screamed. 'These cramps in my stomach! Oh no! Please to God, no! Ohhhh! Ahhhhhhh! No-ohhhhh!'

He died more vividly than anyone, his stomach in his left hand and his cleaver in his right. He rolled his good eye towards the black heavens and fell lengthwise behind a coil of rope.

Maybe, if I had been Livy, if I'd been able to read stars, I'd have seen a conjunction of planets that spelt out this catastrophe. Strange events would have taken place all over the world and I'd have recorded them if I hadn't been here

on this ship at this time in this ocean and my eyes full of
this. I have never been able to use the stars for anything
but navigation and I don't understand them at all. On that
ship in that night I understood nothing, but saw it all,
slowly, in a dream of terror.

The watch had died where he watched. His face held the
agony of death, staring at me with hatred and accusation.
The ship drifted with a dead man at the wheel. Half-Done
Dan made his way in the silence of his own fear. I can see
every inch of that stricken vessel, lit by the moon and its
own nightmare. We sat with our backs against the gunwales
and avoided each other's glances.

Two of them, still alive, came up on to the deck with
cutlasses drawn. They'd been the last to eat and still felt
nothing of the poison that was in them. They saw the Black
Cook stretched out behind his coil of rope. They saw the
two of us, cowering.

'What's happening?'

'We're all dying,' I said. 'It's a plague.'

'Have you poisoned us?'

'We're all dying,' I repeated.

'I wish I was a-dying,' said Half-Done Dan and even in
my fear I could have killed him for it.

'What d'you know about it?'

'Everyone dies on his own desolate shore.'

'You'll die,' said one of them, waving his cutlass, before
which I flinched, but Dan stared back, unmoved.

'What d'you bastard know then?' said the other one, as
they turned their attention to me.

'I'm only seeing what you can,' I said, but I wasn't telling
the truth, because I could see the Black Cook moving, the
great cleaver in his hand, lifting himself from behind his
coil of rope.

'I think it's a plague come down on us. We're going to die
and the ship will drift with its stinking cargo of flesh on to

the rocks of a desolate shore and the sides of it will spill open on the rocks and our bodies will wash on the sands of despair, white and black, dead and cursed through all eternity,' I said, raising my voice to a crescendo to mask any sound of my master.

'What . . . ?'

The Black Cook lifted the blade and brought it down, splitting the skull of one of them. The other turned round, suddenly aware of what was happening, but I leapt on to his sword arm and held it. I had been trained well as a butcher's assistant. He turned on me, trying to extricate his hand, his head switching between us and his eyes realizing that it was already too late.

'No . . .' he screamed, his hand still pulling against my grip. He knew he was already dead and turned to look me in the face rather than see the moment of death as it came and it came quickly, although I saw it all so slowly as it happened and he still stared at me, even though he'd already fallen and his head hung lifeless, face slumped towards the deck and the only thing that was holding him up at all was the grip of my hands around his.

'He was dead, anyway,' said the Black Cook.

'Yes,' I said, letting go.

'They may leave, now.'

'What?'

'They may leave the city. They may take with them the clothes they are wearing. They must go unarmed. They may take with them the memories of their wives and children. Everything else is left behind. They must go now.'

'What?' I was lost.

He indicated the two bodies at our feet, the other bodies on deck and the further bodies unseen in the cabin and below decks. He smiled.

'Throw them overboard, William. They are sailors. They belong in the sea.'

58

Dan and I dragged the bodies one by one to the side of the ship and heaved them over, into the water. The Black Cook bound the wheel and then sat in the cabin that was now his, consulting charts by the light of a lamp. He looked at us for a moment as we came to remove the bodies that shared the cabin with him, but returned to his business without speaking.

The sun was just beginning to rise as we watched the last body splash into the light swell, plunge down and then come back up, half floating, half sinking in the half-light of dawn. The bodies spread out from the ship, some face upward, some down, according to how they fell and how the waves took them. They were caught in the pattern they made with the reflections of the red sun on the sea.

'Release the slaves.' The Black Cook had joined us. He was wearing the Captain's cloak and a three-cornered hat that had belonged to one of the representatives of the Company. He stood beside us, watching the floating dead.

I opened the hatches. I unshackled them. They crawled past me and over each other, climbing on to the deck. They stared at the sun, as if it were a strange god. They hung over the side of the ship and gazed at the unearthly sight of their captors bobbing in the gentle movements of the ocean. In the grey light, their darkness seemed ghostly. The dead in the sea seemed closer to life than these bodies, whose faces were blank with incomprehension; than these bodies that had become air in the stillness of the morning. The dead in the sea had come from the nation of the living and these slaves had crawled from the nation of the dead. They were travelling in different directions and neither had adapted to the change in their circumstances.

SEVEN

THE BLACK COOK TRANSLATES

Let us put him in the scales: Hannibal.
What adds he up to now, the great general?
This is the man for whom vast Africa
Was too small, stretching from the far
Wave-lapped shores of sweet Maroc, ever
Eastward, till she should find that steamy river,
Mighty Nile; find the tribes of Ethiopia
And the Land of Elephants. Listen now and hear
How Spain shall swell his empire of desire.
Behold him! Still he climbs and ever higher.
The Pyrenees behind, see that head now rise
In Alpine passes. Their rocky thighs
Are swathed in blizzards, robed in thunder:
Before his pride they open! split asunder!
The earth moves for Hannibal. Fair Italy
Spread before him, cries upon his mercy.
'Mercy?' Still he pushes on. 'Withdraw?
We have but started. There is more
Shall come: a monstrous force to penetrate
The citadel of Rome; break down her gates
And plant our standard deep and deep and here
In the fecund soils she waters with her tears.'

The Black Cook savoured the triumph of his hero for a moment. He stood up from the Captain's table and moved about the cabin with a perceptible swagger. He turned in a moment and launched himself into a sneering attack on the three-cornered hat that lay innocently on the table-top.

> O what a sight! What subject for a satire!
> The one-eyed chieftain perched on his monster!
> Alas and alack for all our hopes of glory:
> What an end was here! Defeat and ignominy:
> The sad and desperate flight into exile;
> And the world stares at this great Hannibal.
> He is so humble: grasps at the servant's lot,
> Sitting at the door of some small-beer despot,
> Somewhere in the East, drinking a bitter cup,
> And waiting for his majesty to wake up.

'This is Juvenal on Ambition, William, the Tenth Satire. The translation is my own. Perhaps I improve on him slightly. He has done his best, but has he conquered the African general? No. Has he not, rather, diminished himself in our eyes? He is defeated by his own admiration. Where is Hannibal now? Ha! Where is his satirist?'

He swung the cloak about his shoulders and picked up the hat. The one-eyed Scipio perched himself defiantly upon his monstrous ambition.

'Withdraw?' He shook his head and I opened the cabin door for him.

EIGHT

'How many?'

They have woken me up, scrabbling across the floor, climbing up the rough wooden legs of this bed, nosing about my body.

'How many died?'

There have been so many deaths. This is a kind of death in itself, the slow rot of unwashed flesh. All these deaths are just parts of my own, which happens bit by bit, not all at once. Parts of me hadn't even been born before the first parts started dying. The skin flakes off as I rub my eyes and leaves my face raw. These little deaths protect me. Many deaths. I can't remember.

'They only count when you can remember them.'

The sea was full of their bodies.

'Thousands?'

Not thousands. In my mind I can now see thousands of sailors floating away from us, most of them face down because the imagination doesn't need faces.

'More than twenty?'

More than twenty.

'As many as fifty?'

Less than fifty.

'More than twenty and less than fifty?'

Twenty-seven. I choose the ones face up among the thousands who are face down.

'Twenty-seven isn't very many.'

There was the slave who was flogged to death. You have to count him. And the ones who were burnt to death in the shack in the port of G—.

'We didn't see them die. They might have escaped.'

As the flames rose around them they woke up to the horror of their situation. They were so heavy with drink they couldn't lift themselves, the flames burning the tables and benches and their hair and faces until their eyeballs exploded in the fierceness of the heat and their screams were trapped behind their roasted tongues and there were ten of them in all.

'Thirty-eight, then. A drop in the ocean.'

'What were their names?' another voice breaks in. They are trying to catch me out.

'Twenty-seven sailors
Sinking all alone:
Name the sinking names
William Bone.'

They are all joining in now. Their voices have become a choir, which rings in my head. Jack Tar, Davy Jones, Tom Thumb, Johannes Fisk the Norwegian . . . John Cod, Joe Halibut, William Whiting, Henry Haddock, Christopher Kipper, Billy Bloater . . . Martin Mullet . . . Jack Sprat . . . There was Dougal McDougall the Scotchman and Patrick O'Patrick the Irishman and there was the Welshman Pugh.

'That's fifteen.'

They were all below decks. Died in their hammocks, they did, or just close by and we had to haul 'em up. The Captain was Captain Crane and the representatives of the Company were Messrs Grabber and Snatchem. The Master was

McMasters and the cabin boy was called Parker. Jack Bean-
stalk in the crows-nest, he fell all the way down to the deck
screaming, bang. Toby Jug, Tommy Kettle, Arthur King and
Walter Raleigh. How could I forget Sir Francis Drake?
Matthew Mark and Lucas John.

'That was twenty-eight.'

Sir Francis Drake was never there. It must have been
another ship. Died in his bed most likely. The last two were
the ones the Black Cook split with his cleaver. All that
blood and the gobbets of their brains. It's the gospel
truth.

I stir myself and scatter them. It is another day.

The Black Cook raised a pistol above his head and discharged it into the air. In this way he secured their attention, standing on the deck in front of the Captain's cabin
that was now his cabin, his legs braced against the gentle
roll of the ship in the early morning, surrounded by slaves
who were no longer slaves, but in the middle of the ocean
were not free either and the babble had been rising as they
explored the boundaries of their new estate. There was
silence and we all looked to him, in the cloak and three-
cornered hat that made him an emperor amongst a half-
naked rabble. He drew out this silence with a considered
appraisal of his people that no one dared to interrupt. He
interrupted it himself.

'Who here understands me?'

Then or now, I make no claims on understanding. I kept
quiet. The slaves spoke in low voices, eyes fixed on their
new captor, words falling from the sides of their mouths
and under their breath, escaping anyway they could from
the stillness of the situation. Dan looked at me. I could see
he feared some new atrocity, but I turned away. Giving my
attention to the grey-black bodies that were beginning to

draw in some colour from the sun, I took up a deliberate position at my master's right hand.

'Can any of you understand my words?'

I looked into their faces, scrutinizing them all, as if I shared my master's concerns; as if I were almost his equal; as if I were his lieutenant. It was not difficult to avoid Dan's face. He was staring over the side of the ship. A voice came forward out of the indistinguishable sounds of their African languages.

'I do,' the voice said. 'I . . . am . . .' He said his name, but it was just a clatter of incompatible consonants held together with too few vowels. Perhaps the sound of this name, which was just confusion in my ears, meant something to the Black Cook. He did not move, but I felt a tension pass through him.

'You shall have a new name, sir.' We waited. 'I shall call you Hanno,' the Black Cook said, at last.

The man, who was now Hanno, repeated the name. Weighing up the situation, he clearly had no way of seeing how things would work out. He smiled a particularly ingratiating smile at the man in the black cloak and the three-cornered hat and lifted his voice:

'My name is Hanno.'

He turned and spoke in an African tongue to those who surrounded him. His new name stood out from the noise of this story being passed between them. Africans do not all speak the same language. There are many different languages there and the people gathered on the deck of *The Pride Of M—* spoke, perhaps, half a dozen different languages and dialects. Hanno spoke his language, translating from the English, and others, who understood that language, translated it into their own. It was a simple story, celebrated in many tongues, of how a man, in the middle of a broad sea, had been delivered from captivity and had been given a new name, which was Hanno.

'My name is Scipio Africanus.'

Hanno had difficulty with this, but after several attempts, it was mastered and passed amongst the people as a new story: the story of their deliverer, who was black like them, but had a name that was difficult to pronounce, but they would have to learn it out of respect and anyway, he had a gun.

'You shall all have new names. We shall build a great city on the shores of a new continent. The city shall be called New Carthage and you are its citizens, but you must all learn to speak in one tongue. This is the language you must speak.'

An uproar of explanation followed. The pitch of their speaking carried questions and answers. Various voices came to the fore as the vision unfolded.

'Not go back?' asked Hanno, at one point, as if clarifying an issue of debate.

'There is no longer any way back,' replied the Black Cook.

'Names?' asked Hanno after another period of debate.

'Everyone will get a new name.' His eye fell on the woman, shown to him by the sailor on the Coast of N—, so long ago now. She was much changed by the circumstances of her captivity, but he recognized her. He beckoned her forward and she came. 'This woman shall be my queen. I name her Dido. She shall be by my side.'

I made room for her at his side, discreetly, raising my head, at the same time, to give the impression that this had not changed my own status.

'Other names will be made known to you. Hanno will give you names. I will give him lists of names and he will hand them out.'

As Hanno spoke to the crowd, he assumed the role of benefactor, handing out imagined names with largesse. I was already taking a dislike to him. A creeping and unexplained resentment came over me, as I stood there, and this is why I didn't question these events. No. Fear was the reason. It was also the Black Cook's commanding power over my imagination. It was all these things. In its extreme forms, madness takes on the appearance of sanity, except that sanity has never had the power to convince anyone of anything. He stood there in his three-cornered hat and his cloak and nobody questioned the new vision he was imposing upon us, except, perhaps, Half-Done Dan, whose face was a counsel of despair turned towards an empty horizon.

'Many of you will be afraid of this ship and the seas that it sails upon. Before those days when you were brought to the shores of the ocean, you did not imagine it, because it had no shape in your eyes. A man cannot imagine a ship such as this from the carved hull of a canoe. This ship, nevertheless, is your only hope of reaching land. If this ship founders upon the wild sea, you will not be remembered. The ocean will swallow up your lives and your stories and you will be nothing. Your survival depends upon me. It depends upon William Bone, here.' I straightened my back to demonstrate a superior kind of dependability. 'It depends upon Half-Done Dan, over there.' Half-Done Dan did not move. 'It depends upon you all. You will be given tasks. You must learn them quickly and carry them out with great care. There will be a reason for everything you are asked to do. You must not question your orders. Anyone who refuses an order will join those bodies floating in our wake. Is this understood?'

The speech took over an hour, as each detail was translated, explained and discussed in the half-dozen languages and dialects, the Black Cook waiting patiently for each burst to subside before continuing. Dido hung her head. She was no longer in the crowd and took no part in trying to determine the meaning of all these words. Perhaps she picked up some of it in the hubbub. Every now and then,

67

she lifted her head slightly and looked up at the Black Cook out of the corner of her eye.

The day was filled with great activity as we struggled to make sailors out of a people for whom the sea, itself, was beyond comprehension. Here, the true worth of Half-Done Dan became clear. He was everything that he had once said to us so long ago: a consummate seaman. He took the wheel and steered the ship to the Black Cook's navigation. The slaves were willing labour, although it was often quicker to do a job yourself and we were lucky not to run before a storm or have to navigate reefs. There was enough genuine terror in a light breeze and gentle waters.

We ran up the fever flag. If a passing ship had seen us and seen the bodies suspended beneath the waves, it would have steered clear, but the bodies were gone now. I couldn't see them. We had passed beyond that death. Ships pass through the seas in my head, where thousands of bodies float. They offer prayers, but keep to their course through the blood-red ocean. They see us through their distant telescopes and choose not to examine the evident madness of our decks.

NINE

Hanno was born for those days. He combined a sly, sideways turn of mind with true qualities of leadership. I am not certain which aspect of the combination I disliked the most. He organized the ex-slaves into working parties and found the party leaders amongst them. Those that weren't needed, he cleared from our paths, setting them about cleaning the hold from the filth of their old slavery. He listened to his orders with a superhuman attention to detail and saw that everything was done according to our wishes. When there was no work, he would give each party new words to learn. He became an avid collector of words, passing on each one with diligence. He would collect names from the Black Cook which he would memorize, for he could not write, and then distribute. He did it in the manner that he had imagined he would from the first, in the way of a favour granted.

I watched him throwing us glances as he went about his work. If our eyes connected, he would smile. I would smile back graciously, letting him know with a slight inclination of the head, that this was by way of being a favour granted too, in the social hierarchy of the new order.

Tutored by the Black Cook, I am attracted to systems and structures. Every structure I ever attempted has failed me. Every building that was ever built will collapse in its own

69

good time. My structures are built without even the most basic of necessary skills. Knowing they will not survive doesn't affect their potency.

The naming of the people started off in Livy with the Carthaginians, Hamilcar, Bomilcar, Hasdrubal, Mago, Barca, Gisgo, but it became impractical. Instead of having half a dozen names, the Carthaginians called half a dozen people by the same name. The Romans were no better, although, being a Roman, Livy was clearly biased towards the supply of a greater number of Roman names. The Black Cook was biased against Rome, however, and so moved on to battles and then rivers. His problem had in fact been evident in the selection of Dido. Male slaves exceeded female slaves to a significant extent, but not to the extent that men predominate in history. It became clear that this was unforeseen. It was a detail in the great plan that had been overlooked. Having embarked on a certain course, I could see that he was now reluctant to retreat. He became irritable. Hanno wouldn't have minded calling a woman Hasdrubal, but it offended the Black Cook's sensibilities. He wouldn't have minded calling a woman Trasimene. It could easily have been a woman's name and a good name, but the Black Cook balked at calling women after battles. Rivers were acceptable and so we had Ebro, for example, but Tiber had already been handed out to a man before the problem had been truly identified.

'Already is Tiber,' said Hanno.

'Yes,' I agreed. 'Tiber was in yesterday's batch.' It was my attraction to the system that let me down. I should not have allowed myself to become involved. Africanus struck out with a sudden fury that knocked me to the ground.

'Well, throw the bastard overboard and we'll have his name back.'

'I give him other name. Yes. Cannae.' Hanno's intercession came out as a solicitous question. I glowered at him

70

with as much dignity as I could muster, but the Black Cook turned away.

'You may do as you wish.'

I picked myself up and sulked for a while, before he summoned me to his side.

'Your father was called Bone because he was a butcher. It was all he was left with after he had sold his wares, but you can sell bones. He sold you, for example. I was given a name by way of a joke. Major James Tulliver called me Scipio Africanus, because I was an African. Scipio Africanus himself, my original, was called so because of the defeat he inflicted on the African general, Hannibal. So you see, William, I am here as the conqueror of myself, which makes me a very reversible character. This is why you saw me hit you just now. I am not unaware of your sensibilities in this matter, however, and I will have Hanno flogged at the first opportunity. He will say that we have run out of rivers and battles and I shall order twenty lashes.'

'Ten would be fine,' I offered, magnanimously.

Hanno was nobody's fool. Wisely, he pushed the matter no further for a while. The new names assumed a kind of status amongst the Africans, however, as do all commodities in short supply, and discontent began to stir in the face of the obvious social inequity. It was with trepidation that Hanno approached the subject again.

'Hail Scipio,' he began, the Black Cook having instructed him early on in the nature of an appropriate address. 'I ask you forgive me now what I begin to say in just a little while if you agree to this or I not say anything at all no sir. Hail.'

'Speak.' Perhaps he had forgotten his promise, or perhaps he was rewarding diplomatic skill.

'Hail Scipio we want the same thing everybody happy no fight everybody not happy hail Scipio want names.'

The Black Cook frowned, but it was in pain more than

71

anger. Hanno, who wasn't certain of the difference, took a precautionary couple of steps backwards.

'I give out my own name, maybe. You just call me Number Four. One, Two, Three . . .' he explained, pointing to the Black Cook, me and Half-Done Dan in order of rank, 'Four,' returning the finger to his own chest with his ingratiating smile.

There was silence. Hanno was trying to preserve social harmony. It would be a foolish act to strike him for it. For myself, I was quite happy for the punishment to increase to thirty lashes. Out of the pain, I saw the signs of anger, now rising in the Black Cook's breast. Forty, perhaps. I kept my mouth firmly shut.

Suddenly, the Black Cook was grinning. Hanno was grinning too, although clearly he didn't understand why. Any moment he could have been just another light meal for the passing monsters of the deep. There had been an intellectual breakthrough, however, of the kind that are the stuff of emperors and not the stuff of historians, who do not face the problems that make such stuff necessary.

'What is your name?' he asked me.

'You know my name,' I answered nervously.

'William Bone.'

'Yes,' studying his face for a clue as to what this might mean.

'Was there a William Bone in Carthage?'

'I'm not sure,' I said, preserving what I perceived as the advantage of a non-committal stance.

'But there will be a William Bone in the New Carthage.'

'Yes,' I agreed triumphantly, unaware of a reason for triumphalism, but glad to see my name amongst the saved.

'The New Carthage shall be an empire in the truest sense, bringing together many peoples. If there is to be a William and a Dan, let us have a Tom, a Dick and a Harry.'

The steps that make a new civilization possible can be breathtakingly simple.

'Tom, Dick, Harry,' repeated Hanno. 'Man or woman's names, Tom, Dick, Harry?'

'They are men's names,' I advised him, looking momentarily to the Black Cook for approval. Nothing was certain any more.

'Woman's names?' Hanno asked tentatively.

'An emperor does not know the names of all his subjects.' It was a breezy reply and signalled the end of the interview. Hanno turned to go, but was called back. 'William is my historian. He can people my history with a thousand names.'

Hanno looked at me and I nodded at him confidently, a thousand names disappearing from my head in an instant.

'Later,' I said.

Hanno was back amongst the Africans. In his absence, some of them had contrived a way into the stores, by means of some loose planking. He pulled out the three instigators, or three who would at least stand as instigators, and had them flogged. Hasdrubal had become the man entrusted with the task of flogging. He had a talent for it; a subtlety in his strength that allowed him to hand out punishment in graduated severity. These were relatively light punishments. The punished knew it and were grateful. Hanno handed out an extra ration of biscuit all round as if to say: 'The stealing of food is a serious misdemeanour, but I am of you and I understand hunger.'

The people were happy and jabbered away to each other, eating their biscuits. Even the punished held on to their biscuits as a token of achievement, although they were still too weak to eat, lying on the deck, their backs tended by four or five of the still unnamed women. Hanno stood over them and motioned the women away. He called the attention of everyone and pointed at the three in turn.

73

'Name Tom. Name Dick. Name Harry.'

There was great acclaim for the action in the strange throat noises of the Africans. There was a genius in Hanno's dealings with people. He was the tireless source of social inspiration that all oppressive regimes have need of and without which all oppressive regimes fall. Hanno could represent imperial will to popular acclaim.

The Black Cook watched the proceedings and made his own mental notes. Half-Done Dan watched the proceedings from the wheel and seemed to take no note of it at all. I watched with admiration. Hanno was a dangerous man. I moved closer to my master and examined the charts he had spread out before him.

'We should see the coast of Q— before too long. Another day. Maybe two. We will turn south. There.'

He pointed to a space on the chart: a line of shore with no other markings. He lifted his finger and indicated from south-west to west-south-west in a broad gesture that incorporated a thousand miles of the unseen coast.

TEN

In the night, Hanno appeared at my cabin door with two women. I looked at him and at them and found myself rising, beneath my breeches. Hanno had a sharp eye and he grinned.

'Give them names Mister William.' He had dispensed with the Hail William as he had grown more confident. 'They want names. What you want? You want one of these? Yours Mister William. Other one for Mister Dan. Which one you want?'

I considered their bodies. One was evidently younger, but not by much. I made a guess at eighteen and, perhaps, twenty years old. The trade had no use for the old, who wouldn't repay their passage. They were in good condition, still a little thin from their privations, but their breasts had a good shape, the younger one's slightly smaller and firmer. It might have been this that made me distinguish between their ages. Their hair, which had been close cropped to their heads when they had boarded, had grown a little, the tight wiry curls of it springy to the touch. The older one had a face that was broader and flatter and her skin was of a deeper hue. I felt their thighs. The older one had the stronger thighs. They both had good strong buttocks after the manner of the African, but the buttocks of the older one were broader. Her whole body was broader and stronger,

75

although, as I say this, I wouldn't want to convey the impression that she was not attractive. She had a strong beauty. And I wouldn't want to convey the impression in all this, that the younger one was frail. She was not, but she had a more compliant beauty. As I looked into the older one's eyes, she engaged mine. It was her face that was older. There were rich movements in her eyes. There was a power in her face, I found myself backing away from.

'Name?' she asked, but I made no answer.

As I looked into the other's face, I saw someone falling out of a tree, who didn't know whether to shut her eyes or keep them open. In the same involuntary way I had found myself rising, I heard myself say, all of a sudden, 'I'll catch you,' but I closed my mouth against the words coming out.

As I lingered over her, my head filled with thoughts of my own Mary, rich jellies and Fat Agatha's hindquarters. I put my hands on her shoulders.

'Mary,' I said and she repeated it.

Hanno clapped me on the back with a procurer's familiarity. He knew my choice without me having to say a thing.

'What we call this one?'

I had been dreading my new responsibilities from the moment that I had been given them. It had been working away in my mind, the names coming slowly on a list. Kings and queens, characters from the stories told to me by the pig-keeper's daughter, characters from Bible stories. I wrote them down and crossed them out and then wrote them in again. Names seemed good and then ridiculous, immediately after. Every name seemed ridiculous. I was preparing for an imagined moment, when I would stand before the assembled crowd and hand them out, one by one, the Africans coming forward. I wanted my names to sound strong and appropriate to a new empire. I had not imagined that it would be done piecemeal, like this. Faced with Mary, I found myself unable to say anything but Mary, but it was like releasing a log from a dammed stream. It was a liberation and I realized that names did not matter at all. People become their names and their names take on the grandeur and humility of their carriers. This was why the Black Cook had grinned at Hanno. He had realized that the road he was upon ended in a stone wall. Break down the wall and you may wander amongst the open hills.

'Alice.' I plucked it out of the air. It had no meaning. It was the first name to fly into my head. 'Alice!'

Hanno repeated it. Alice repeated it. Hanno clapped me on the back again and led her off.

'I called you Mary,' Mary repeated her name, 'after another Mary,' she picked out the name again and echoed it back, 'a childhood sweetheart,' I said. 'You made me think of her, but in a way I am always thinking of her and what happened to her. I will never know, Mary.' Again, she said the name and I indicated my pleasure at her response. 'Like you, I was torn from my home and sold into a kind of slavery and though it was not slavery, there was no way back from it. There is never a way back. If I had not been torn from my home, would I have married Mary? And if I had married Mary, would we have found our way back to the smoking shed? Mary, you and I, Mary, have fallen from trees. We are both rushing headlong towards the ground. You don't understand, so I can speak to you. If I taught you a thousand words, you would understand me, but it wouldn't stop us falling.'

'Mary,' she said. She understood more than her name. She understood her situation. She removed the bit of cloth that was tied around her hips.

THE BLACK COOK ON EMPIRE

Empire is the conquest of finite space, measured in land, across the continents of the Earth, and in the sea that lies between them.

The impulse towards Empire lies in the circle of the visible world. Within that circle we can imagine ourselves owning all that we see or alternatively we can imagine ourselves as a kind of insect. These are the twin poles of the human response: power and insignificance. The impulse to Empire is sexual.

Empire is experienced in the flow from an emperor downwards. It exists in the congress of a man with a woman and can be imagined as that. We see a flow from that greater accretion of power to the weaker: thus, Empire is an ordering of the world according to natural laws.

Empire is bound by no other law than that of sustainable oppression. Without oppression, there is no Empire: thus, it is discovered, oppression is the natural order of the world.

Strength is Nature's greatest gift. In that Empire is the distribution of great strength, it is that greatest of generosities, Love. The strategies of Empire and Love are the same: they are strategies of enlargement.

Enlargement is the destiny of an emperor. He gazes upon the fertile plain as upon a woman and she opens herself to him. Finite space is a fertile plain, Time is the emperor's enemy and History is his weapon.

The Black Cook's philosophical systems filled my thoughts as I explored this woman who had come within the circle of my visible world; as I moved across her continents and seas, taking possession of her in my own name and in the name that I had given her; feeling her as she moved according to my requirements on the floor of the cabin that had once belonged to the representatives of the Company, but was now mine.

'Mary,' I said in imperial exhilaration.

'Mary,' she answered in submission to the fleets in her

harbours and the armies lined up on her shores, but I was not an admiral or a general. I was an historian, watching an empire rise and fall, its once mighty borders shrinking to their point of origin and even further. There was nothing more to say and I found myself disturbed by her inability to reply with more than her name. I pointed to the floor beneath my hammock and indicated that she could lie there.

I could not sleep and took out my fiddle, passing the night in sad, slow airs. I played, for the most part, with my eyes closed, but I always knew that she was listening. Lying on the floor of the cabin she watched me play. She watched my face, lost in the tunes. Tears gathered in her eyes. This cheered me up, although I did not show it. A good audience is another kind of empire.

Only one or two rats remain and those are intent on finding small insects in the crevices between the flagstones. One of them looks at me, realizing I am taking a pause in the narrative.

'What did it smell like? We like a bit of bumbo, but you've got to give us something we can get our noses into. Pokey in the poke hole. Give us something we can get our teeth into. What did it taste like? If rats went on like that, they'd have died out years ago.'

I am trying to remember what it tasted like. I am trying to remember the smell. I can remember the smell of sour milk, but that came later. Her skin tasted of the salt of lost oceans, the sweat dried on to her skin, concentrated in the hollows under her arms, as my lips closed around her nipples that were so deep and so dark a brown they were purple beneath the rough edge of the brown, my nostrils took the scent rolled in waves across my face and my face plunged down beneath the waves, down and down and my tongue

79

found the salts of a deeper sea, alive with vegetation and fish swimming in amongst the weeds and it was as if the whole continents of her body had risen from these depths, carrying their memory of true salt, flecked now across her brown earth and dried in the sun. A man couldn't live in such depths, opening his eyes so far beneath the waves, he would see a different world defined by the element of water through which bubbles of air escaped from his mouth and he would try to swim, holding his breath, lungs packed tight against his ribcage, gasping as he hauled himself ashore.

Was it like that? Or was that later too?

My question is ignored, but a few more rats have gathered. Maybe it was like that. It was like that.

Alice sat on the deck, a few feet from the wheel, at which Half-Done Dan did his best to ignore her presence. Mary had risen dutifully, as I'd left the cabin, and she followed me. The sun was half-way out of the sea and I was feeling happy.

'It's a fine morning, Dan,' I offered, but he would countenance no optimism.

'The weather means nothing to a hanged man.'

His customary depression had moved towards a deeply morbid melancholy. 'When we've done our job, he'll have us swinging from the yardarm,' he used to say. 'No,' I used to answer with an uncertain bravado.

'Another few days and we'll make land,' I said, but he was locked into his own concerns.

'He'll not like whiteys. Can't say I blame him, but it's not much use to the likes o' you and me. He'll want to live with his own. Stands to reason. And even if he doesn't do it himself, this lot'll murder us in our sleep soon as look at us. That little bastard Hanno has put one here to spy on me. Turn my back and she'll probably pull a knife out of her arse and have me. Most likely we'll swing though.'

'She hasn't got a knife. I'll hold the wheel for you. Get yourself a bit.'

'They'll want her back when they see how few women there are to go around. They'll pull me out of her with a rope round my neck. Have you ever seen a one-legged man hang? He can't even struggle properly. It's all one-sided and he starts going round in circles. I'm too old for it.'

'Land ahoy!' sang out Bomilcar in the crows-nest. The Black Cook burst from his cabin with his charts, followed by Dido carrying his cloak and hat. He scanned the horizon for a confirmation of the sighting. Word travelled through the ship in all the different languages and the citizens gathered to catch a sight of their coastline.

'We're as good as hanged,' said Half-Done Dan.

The Black Cook came back through the ship and stood with us. He raised his voice to address the people.

'In a week, he has hardly slept. He has steered this ship towards safety; safety and a new country. We owe him our lives.'

Hanno translated and was retranslated and they broke out in their African cheering, many of them before the translation had reached their ears. Alice stood up and said something to the crowd in her own language and this was passed around to more cheers until it reached us: 'The man with one leg cares so much, he will not leave this wheel even when a woman opens her legs.'

The cheers were laughter and we all laughed together when everybody realized we all understood the same thing. Some of them started singing and dancing on the deck at the thought of land and the thought of the man who cared for them this much. The Black Cook clapped his arm round Dan, who would have been dwarfed within such a grip, anyway, and now shrank further, but even in the midst of these celebrations, the Black Cook was thinking of destiny

81

and was giving precise instructions for the new course. We sailed still and in the general happiness, everyone wanted to work towards our expected landfall and Hanno and I were kept busy finding jobs for them all.

We were a nation in a bottle and I thought often of Dan's philosophy. It was a nation pulling together and growing in the fair breeze. No matter how desolate the shore, we could build on it and I was filled with hope for our prospects. In the moments when I was not working, I would retire to my cabin with Mary and play her music. She would smile at the hornpipes and cry with the slow airs. Either served to put her in the mood for rolling. If I felt well satisfied, I would teach her words and she applied herself to them dutifully.

Dan kept to the wheel, as ever. I did not speak to him much in those days, for his gloomy disposition found no place in my breast, but I noticed that he had begun to let Alice hold the wheel sometimes. She would have held anything for him, but he rarely looked at her much and never asked for anything. He would motion her to the wheel, though, when he became too tired to continue and he would grab snatches of sleep. I was grateful to see him taking the rest, for his eyes had taken on a wild visionary quality. He did not seem to see people at all at these times, rather he saw through them to the desolate shores that approached closer by the day.

We were only a few miles out from the coast now, following the line of it south. The Black Cook was constantly engaged in consulting charts, comparing them with the corresponding hills and plains and villages and the mouths of rivers that could be seen by all of us, but picked out in detail through his telescope. Hanno would constantly climb between the deck and the crows' nest asking a particular question of the look-out and then returning with his answer to the Black Cook, who would then be prompted to ask another question that would send Hanno scurrying back up the rigging.

It was a surprise, one evening, to see Alice alone at the wheel, holding it in the proud, stiff way that she did. I looked around and saw Dan standing aft and looking over the side. He knew I had approached him, but he didn't turn round.

'Don't want to see that desolate shore, Will. Ships are all I know.'

'Nations in bottles,' I said, not really knowing what to say.

'Mine was poured over the side. Empty. Nothing left at all.'

I thought he was still worrying about being murdered in his sleep and tried to comfort him. 'You are respected, Dan. You are their saviour. Alice would murder anyone who threatened a hair on your head. I will look after you in the new world.'

He didn't seem to be listening, but suddenly laughed. 'You?'

I couldn't find an answer. I didn't want to talk to him any more. I wanted to find Mary and feel a part of a great enterprise again. I was angry with him for steering me on to rocks, when the open sea beckoned in every other direction.

'I'm going over the side,' he said.

It was my turn to laugh. 'What?'

'I'm going to swim for it.'

'You'll never make the coast and even if you did, you'd not survive.'

'Don't want to reach no coast. Don't want to reach anything. Want to reach nothing, Will. I want to reach something as empty as an empty bottle. I'll swim round in circles until there's no hope left in my heart and then I'll drown and I'll be nothing and all of this shithole of a life will disappear behind me.'

I put my arm on his back to comfort him, but he threw me a look of such reproach that I stepped back. He hoisted himself up and swung himself over the gunwales, pausing for a moment only to stare into my face with his wild eyes, as if I was trying to stop him, but I couldn't move, trapped in a kind of disbelief that saw it all so slowly but so impossible to engage in. He dropped into the water, down through the surface that closed rapidly above him and then up again. He turned on to his stomach and swam.

I stood transfixed. I tried to detect the wider pattern of his movement, but I couldn't see the arc that I longed for. Wild flurries of activity would send spirals of turbulent foam out from his arms, his good leg, his wooden one. There was no equality in any of it, such circles as there were disappeared in the surrounding greater movements of the waves.

Others gathered, staring over the side of the ship. Alice saw the commotion and the pointing and then saw the bizarre thrashings of the swimmer with a wooden leg. She abandoned the wheel and rushed to where I was standing. She tried to climb over the gunwales, as if to join him, but she didn't struggle as I pulled her back and held her. We watched.

As he approached an imagined death, perhaps his sense of purpose was not strong enough to create the great circle he had envisaged, or perhaps I was being distracted by a true course's minor variations, which would, taken over a sufficient scale, be seen to cancel each other out. Each flurry would be followed by a period of collapse, where he simply drifted with the sea. And sometimes he swam on his back taking the projected curvature of despair in the opposite direction. Right hand veering placed against left hand veering, he was quite possibly swimming in a straight line. As we stood there, Alice and I, my arms around her waist and, even in the sadness of the occasion, an undeniable erection

84

pressing through my breeches against her strong buttocks, for a while I thought that this might be the case and I imagined Dan smiling at the discovery of it in his breast, but I was taking no account of the irregular periods of drift where he was abandoned to the will of the ocean. There was no pattern, or rather none that I could see. If hope was a straight line and despair a circle, and I thought for a moment of the fact that the pressure of my body flattened a kind of circle in Alice's buttocks and my erection was a kind of hopeful straight line, then I saw Dan swimming hopeless and despairless every movement cancelling out the previous without being forced into its opposite. It was a kind of freedom. Perhaps it was the nothing that he had talked of, the random movements of which reflected patterns beyond human comprehension. My hands moved up between her breasts, whether to comfort her heart or mine, I didn't know. It took such a long time.

'He'll reach no shore.' The Black Cook stood behind me. He had given Hanno temporary charge of the wheel.

'He's trying to swim in a circle.' I didn't believe it any more, but I wanted to protect Dan from the indignity of a futile attempt at escape.

'Why?'

'He wants to prove to himself that there is no hope before he dies.'

'He doesn't need proof.' But we all need proof and all we ever get is inadequate explanation drowning in contradictions, yet still trying to swim.

'No,' I said. The Black Cook spat over the side.

'He served his purpose. You'll have to take over the wheel, William. Keep the woman there to help you.'

I stood at the wheel with Alice beside me and Mary beside her. Mary had brought my fiddle and after a few hours, I picked it up, motioning Alice to take over. Sitting on the deck, I composed a lament, which I called *Dan Done and*

Drowned. It took half an hour to get it the way I wanted it and then I played it, Mary listening with her eyes fixed intently on the bowing and the movement of my fingers and Alice listening, staring forward with the direction of the ship. I played it, imagining my friend floating upside down, his white hair caught in weeds, his empty eyes amongst the fish and his wooden leg sticking up, bobbing in the waves. Though I could explain nothing, they knew what I was playing and the tears flowed freely. For good or ill, we were three now. I was their protection and they recognized in me a man who hadn't been able to prevent a cripple throwing himself overboard. Perhaps this was what they drew on in the tears that welled up in their eyes. Perhaps this was the real reason for my own tears and Half-Done Dan was still swimming with nobody left to mourn the fact that he was still alive.

ELEVEN

THE STORY THAT ALICE TOLD

His name was Two-World Dan, because he lived across the border between this world and the spirit world of our ancestors and he had a leg in each camp. In this world, they called him Half-Finished, because they could see that one of his legs had already crossed the border, but in the world of the ancestors, he was known as Hardly-Started. Where we saw a wooden leg, the ancestors saw a wooden man with only this one leg as spirit flesh and blood. When he travelled in the world of the ancestors, he became wooden in this world. Beautiful women would open their legs to him, for they saw in his face a great traveller who had undergone the terrors of another world, but his eyes were as of wood and he did not see them and his thing, itself, was almost wooden and did not move. It was dangerous to travel in the other world, for the longer he stayed, the more he turned into a carving of a man. He travelled in the other world, because he sought the advice of the ancestors.

'Two-World Dan,' asked one of the ancestors, seeing him on the road one day, his wooden face searching the terrain for the right direction, 'when will you settle here? Two-World Dan, is it not time you came across?'

Two-World Dan answered him: 'I will live here when I am not needed there.'

'Who needs you in that world?' asked the ancestor.

'A people cast upon the waves of a great ocean need me. Show me the right road that we must follow, for the right road in your world, is a path through the oceans of their world, just as a path through your seas is a journey across their continents: show me this road and I shall come across. My body shall be a piece of driftwood in their world and you shall see all of me in the spirit flesh and blood here.'

The ancestor pointed in the direction of a sweet valley, its slopes covered in flowers and trees bearing fruits that were exquisite in their colours. A river ran through the valley, bringing water to the fields that grew fine crops, and it seemed a place of great peace and harmony.

'You have tried to trick me,' said Two-World Dan. 'In their world, that peaceful valley will be mountainous waves and that sweet river will be the rocks on which their ship would founder. I will take that road leading across the plains, because your plains are their calms. In the distance I can see the barren shores of a dead sea and it is towards that fertile land I will steer their ship.'

The ancestor smiled, which was his way of showing anger. 'Two-World Dan,' he said, 'trick or no trick, you must come across, for I have shown you the way in which you must steer their ship.'

'I will come across,' said Two-World Dan, 'but, because you have tried to trick me, I will still be Two-World Dan and if that people cast upon the waves of the ocean need me, I will return to them.'

The ancestor laughed a howl of anguish, because he knew that Two-World Dan had had the better of him and no ancestor likes to be beaten by the living. In this world, the people cast upon the waves of the ocean saw Two-World Dan throw himself into the sea and as he swam, he moved less and less as he became a piece of driftwood, but in that other world, there was a joy in his heart as he travelled through those sweet lands he had seen for what they were.

This was the story that Alice told and it passed amongst the Africans with subversive tenacity. A group of them took to gathering round her as she held the wheel. Some had never recovered from the shock of their enslavement. They had a look of perpetual simplicity about them. They would work willingly, but were not of much use. These, in particular, gathered at Alice's feet, to listen to the stories she delivered in her singsong voice.

Her skill was evident. Even though I could take nothing from it, each word lapped at the shores of everything I have ever understood. Each note in her voice said: 'Listen!' Why had I not chosen her? But she seemed to harbour no resentment. Had she always told these stories? Had she told them in Africa? I imagine her telling stories in the hold of the ship, chained to the smell of piss and shit, but it is painful. If she was here now, I wouldn't be telling this story, but my grey hairs would be on her shoulders and my lips on her neck and even though the wood has turned soft below decks and she might no longer be as young as I remember her, I would spend my life breaking up in her seas.

Hanno, it was, of course, who first translated the story. When the Black Cook heard it, he became violently angry. Alice, who stood proudly at the wheel, refused to deny anything and he ordered her flogged. He told the Africans, if anyone was heard repeating the story, they too would be flogged.

Alice was tied to the mast and Hasdrubal flogged her. We all watched. I watched with a film across my eyes, for I

89

didn't want to see, but even in that blur I could see each stroke coming down on the back that I had pressed against, my hands between her breasts, feeling the beat of her heart as we watched Dan in the water. Hasdrubal made a great show of ferocity in the punishment, but in reality each stroke was as restrained as he was able to make it. Alice had the respect of all the Africans. They were a little afraid of her. Though it was clear there was more than a little resentment at the way the turn of events had provided me with two women, when they had so few, they never moved against the situation.

When the flogging had finished, I indicated to Mary that she should take Alice to the cabin. I told Hanno to organize a couple of people to carry her there. He looked to the Black Cook for approval, but it was not necessary. Slowly, Alice stood up, held up her head and made her own way, Mary following behind. The Africans cleared a path for her. Hanno did not like to be caught like this, in the open, between conflicting forces, but the conflict was not as severe as it seemed. The Black Cook's anger had become policy. He had spoken to me discreetly before the flogging: 'Keep her in the cabin for a few days and keep her busy.' When I ordered Hanno to see to the wheel, he was glad to be given the job.

I took a bucket of sea water through to tend Alice's wounds.

TWELVE

It's not the first time I've written this. In former days I would store the pages beneath my bed, but so many of them went for nests. Some I have rewritten, but it's not the same. Some of them are lost forever. I don't blame the rats. They are only acting after their nature. They don't read and don't mind what order I read things to them. They don't mind if an episode changes and they don't mind if an episode gets lost. I could read them the same episode every day and they would go on about their business. If they question something, they only speak as they find things on a particular day. Sometimes, when I am wholly engrossed in it, they lose interest completely. Sometimes, when I rattle along with an almost negligent air, their noses twitch upon my every word. And then, when I might try to rattle along with an assumed negligence, they neglect me completely and I pace my cell with strident apathy trying to recount my story to the occasional head that pokes briefly from a hole in the wall before turning round and disappearing. And then again, I might be so absorbed in the paper in front of my eyes, writing furiously and reading the words out loud as they come, half-word by half-word, phrase by phrase, recaptured picture by recaptured picture, that I do not even notice when they climb the table legs to chew the pages as I write.

I have a patron. When I started, I wrote for you, Major James Tulliver, in the knowledge that it was you who gave orders for the regular supply of paper and ink. When I asked for a metal box to protect my work from the rats, I imagined you saying, yes, this should be supplied without delay, because it came within only a year or more of my asking. It sits on the table and when I finish writing for a day, I gather up my papers, open it up and put them in. Sometimes, I go through them and take out duplicated episodes, offering them to the rats freely, as a conciliatory gesture, guilty at the imperious way in which I might have brushed them from my table the day before.

'Write that history, Mr Bone. I should be very interested to read that history. You will write it for me. It is not a history for the world's ears.'

I was glad to do anything that might find favour. I don't know if you are still waiting. I haven't liked to ask and the gaoler will not speak to me, anyway. Perhaps, when I have finished this history, you will read it and burn it and I will swing from the gallows. You will place it back in the metal box and strike a spark to all this paper and my history will die with me. Even though I shall not be entirely dead, my story will be. Perhaps you left this island long ago. Perhaps the rats are my patrons, now. A man must speak to somebody. Their voracious appetite for stories, ordered chronologically or not, shapes my labour. Have I become frightened of finishing? It all takes so long. I am like Half-Done Dan. I write as he swam, with a wooden leg to keep me afloat in a sea of possibilities, searching for complete emptiness. If these pages are a kind of empire, I would want them to be an empire without hope or despair.

THIRTEEN

If stories could be got rid of with a good flogging, the world would be a better place for it, but Two-World Dan now lived in the lines across Alice's back and though the raw red stripes scabbed over, Two-World Dan was an infection that would not let them heal. I had Mary wash Alice's back three times a day with sea water, Alice with her teeth gripping a length of rope as the salts etched themselves into the raw flesh. She did not complain. She spoke to no one. It would be clear to anybody that she was not responsible for this story of hers, but she walked about the ship. I could not stop her, short of tying her down, and the story went with her. She said nothing, but the Africans read the lines across her back. The page changed each day with new textures of scabbing and infected sores. As the scar tissue eventually knotted together in fixed ridges and troughs, so the story became fixed in the consciousness of the city of New Carthage and its citizens.

It was five days after the flogging that we found the river mouth which the Black Cook had been searching for. He talked of it in those terms, as if it had been lost and he would recognize it as soon as we came across it. It was unnamed on the charts, but later I heard it called R—. He needed the Carthaginians to believe that their country was a specific place, a promised land. Sometimes I caught a

93

glimpse of collapse in his eye. The white walls of his city would fall headlong into the foaming sea. He would cheer himself up with a flogging, rebuilding it with each stroke. I could usually see such moods coming upon him, but the Carthaginians could not. Dido could read his moods and sometimes she would lead him to his cabin and, there, rebuild his city, who knows?

He had been searching for that river mouth or any river mouth, any natural harbour that had not been discovered by any other emperor, or if it had been discovered, had been abandoned. He had searched, balancing civic requirements against the growing impatience of the citizenry. And so we steered our ship into the protection of this river's deep channel. The Black Cook took the wheel and I swung the lead for him. No one else could be trusted.

It was a brown river. No. It was yellow. It was between these colours, full and thick with sediments washing down towards the sea. Crocodiles basked on its mudbanks and islands. The natural borders of land and water were ignored in this country with trees colonizing the shallow reaches of the river, their roots deep in the riverbed and the river finding a flood plain across miles of low-lying forest. Branches would hang down towards the water with strange fruits and vines, and fish watched us from the banks.

A group of Indians watched our arrival. They seemed neither surprised nor welcoming. Their faces registered neither pleasure nor displeasure. When we called to them, they didn't react, but they stood in the rain, watching. The Carthaginians chattered amongst themselves, in obvious high spirits at seeing this third race of people, at least half of whom were women.

A landing party was formed: Hanno, Hasdrubal, Bomilcar, Tom, Dick and Harry. Each was armed with a musket, in the use of which the Black Cook had been training them. I rowed, with a pistol in my belt. The Black Cook carried

94

two pistols. He came ashore like any discoverer, clambering on to dry land, but standing up immediately and with as much dignity as could be mustered. In his three-cornered hat and black cloak, he took possession of the territory. He didn't say anything, but he didn't need to. He assumed an imperial air that grew with each step. The landing party of Carthaginians were visibly affected by the steadiness of the earth beneath their feet. They held their guns at the surrounding countryside and we followed our emperor as he walked towards the savages.

One of them came forward and offered me his hand. I shook it, but indicated the greater importance of my master. The Indian seemed confused for a moment, but then quite readily offered his hand to the Black Cook. He then shook hands with the bodyguard, who looked at each other and at their hands, themselves confused at this formality. Others came forward and we spent a few minutes making sure that everyone had shaken hands with everybody else.

Their leader pointed out in the direction of the ocean, jerking his head after his arm with a questioning expression.

'Yes,' the Black Cook nodded vigorously, 'we have come over the great ocean in our ship. We are New Carthaginians. That is our ship, in which we crossed the mighty waves of the Atlantic. We have sailed for many weeks.'

The Indian listened politely and when the Black Cook had finished, smiled understanding. He used his finger to draw a circle in the air that seemed to include the entire landing party and then he pointed north.

'No,' said the Black Cook. He pointed to a hill rising above the river. 'We shall settle there. That hill shall be the city of New Carthage.'

The Indian was confused by this. He talked to his companions for a moment and then came back to his circling. He held up his five fingers many times and pointed to the barrels of the muskets, drawing great flowers in the air

95

coming out of them. He made as if to fall over dying with his hands over his stomach and then pointed his finger at each of his companions in turn and they did the same. He had broken into an animated explanation of the story, pointing north and pointing at me. Then he stood up and came towards me again. He held out his hand and we shook hands again. He circled his companions and himself and pointed south.

'As the Emperor of New Carthage, I offer you my protection. You may walk in peace in these lands.'

The Indian pointed south again and spoke to the others, who lifted their burdens and prepared to follow him. The Black Cook put his hand on the low savage shoulder and fixed the man with his eye.

'We would have food and water.' He made signs for eating and drinking and was met with laughter. The Indian spoke a few words to his companions and they all laughed. With a broad sweep of his arm, he indicated the river and the surrounding countryside, laughing again. The Black Cook became angry and pointed a pistol at the Indian's head. The laughter stopped and they fell on the muddy earth. humiliating themselves at our feet, in the rain, for it had been raining all this time without cease.

The Black Cook drew the frightened man up out of the mud and signalled that all was forgiven. He took a piece of gold out of a purse he carried at his belt and gave it to the Indian. With a broad gesture of his arm, he indicated the extent of the land he considered now purchased by him and laughed. The Indian laughed nervously, looking at the gold coin and testing it between his teeth. The others got up slowly and picked up their possessions again.

We all laughed together, in the rain, each of us reading the situation in our different ways and each of us finding some humour in it. Tom, Dick and Harry moved towards the women, who had stayed in the background during these exchanges. Dick singled out one of them and tried pulling her towards our positions.

'Tell him if he wants her,' the Black Cook explained to Hanno, 'he can have her here in the mud and the rain and I will wait until he has finished and when he has finished I will blow his brains out.'

Hanno explained and Dick let go of her. She rejoined the Indians as quickly as Tom and Harry had rejoined Bomilcar and Hasdrubal, who laughed because they had their own women on the ship. Dick did not move for a few moments. It appeared that he had let go of the woman in response to orders, but it was equally possible that he had let go in order to get a proper grip on his musket, for he spun round suddenly with a wild anger in his eyes. The discharge of the Black Cook's pistol dropped him to the ground. The ball had gone through his temple even before he had fully turned. We all stood for a while dazed by the turn of events. The Indians had tears in their eyes and the woman approached Dick's body, squatting beside him with an expression of exquisite pity on her face. She was joined by the others, all their faces filled with pity for the stranger from across the seas, who had died for love.

Perhaps I am imagining some of this. Could I have seen tears in all that rain? We stood in the rain. It dripped from the three-cornered hat, from our noses, from our chins. It ran down our faces. Or maybe we were all crying. But it dripped from the trees. It fell on the surface of the river and on the naked bodies of the Indians and on the gold coin that their leader still held between two fingers and the thumb of his right hand, having nowhere in particular to put it unless he unwrapped his basket of possessions. Their expression was perhaps more fear and wonder than pity. The rain worries me, because I can see it when I picture that strange meeting, but when the Black Cook speaks, I do not see rain. It must have rained. It rained so much on that

97

coast. When I hear our voices, however, I do not hear them raised above the sound of the rain. Perhaps it is just another historian trying to keep his history dry so that the ink will not run. Add your own rain to New Carthage and you will never match the water that could fall from those skies.

In amongst their tears, if they were crying, the Black Cook moved suddenly and pulled out Dick's woman. He gave her to Tom. With a pistol raised, he pulled out another woman for Harry.

With a commanding thrust of his arm, he indicated that the Indians should continue south and they did. The two women followed them with their eyes, but said nothing. They came without complaint in the longboat and stood without complaint on the deck of the ship while the Carthaginians examined them. They disappeared in the night, while Tom and Harry slept. No one saw them leave or heard them, but they must have been long gone when it was realized. It was a cause of great laughter, to all but Tom and Harry, who became known as men next to whom the snakes of the forest were an improvement.

FOURTEEN

If I have difficulty with the rains, it is because they washed so much away, dragging the soil from the cleared forest down, along with our feeble attempts at crops, down into the yellow-brown mud of the river. There was so much rain, it seems improbable that I can see the burning of that city state at all. The flames and the rain should cancel each other out. I find things harder and harder to remember, the closer I come to the present. But if I cannot remember it, why am I here? There must have been days when it didn't rain. Now that I think of it, there were hundreds of days when it didn't rain and it must have been on one of those that I saw flames.

New Carthage, you were a sorry mistake. The pain comes from recognizing that you did exist and that there is a difference between something carved in the imagination and something hewn from the virgin forest. If there was not, nothing would protect us from the imagination of our neighbours and so little does.

The Black Cook had made me see what he saw and it was a white city. At the top of a rounded hill stood a palace, and the broad avenues ran down from it with a kind of geometrical precision. Beyond the walls of the city, fields spread out with golden wheat tall in the sunlight. Roads ran from the gates of the city to all points of the known world and along these roads, traders would bring the exotic wares of distant civilizations. They would be hailed by farmers straightening their backs in the rich fields and greeted as they came to the city walls by guards from an army that was confident in its strength and could afford to show hospitality, joking and passing comments in a rough good humour on the goods they carried. As they made their way slowly up the broad avenues, between the fine white plaster walls of the well-appointed houses, they would marvel at the easy contentment of New Carthage; its happy citizens; its benevolent emperor, who would accommodate them in the many rooms of the palace, where music could be heard at all times and succulent dishes would be brought from the kitchens. Sometimes, the emperor himself would even cook dishes and they would be of an unsurpassed sweetness, for he had once been a cook, many years ago, before he had come to this throne. He had been known as the Black Cook. He would laugh as sweetly as he cooked and they would carry tales of this noble city across the oceans of the world. New Carthage was a source of fabled wonder.

He could make you see things that weren't there; that should be there. It was like crossing a border. A step on a dusty road and you are in another country. You crossed the border into his lands and these things were there. Everything was indeed as he saw it and he had banished fear.

There were roads, or rather, tracks through the forest. We were never truly isolated. Tales found their way north and south along the coastline and west into the interior. Word of an African kingdom certainly reached hundreds of miles to the north, to the slave plantations. Our numbers increased with runaways, although work in New Carthage cannot have been less arduous than on the plantations themselves. There was a constant movement of Indians travelling in all directions away from the European settlements: families; small groups; whole tribes of dispossessed. And there were the Indians who were native to the forests of New Carthage. They would sometimes visit us with food to trade for any strange rarity we would be content to part with. Our labours were a source of wonder to them. They could see no reason for it, animals, fish, fruits, nuts and edible roots being all around us in great plenty. We learnt from their abundant knowledge of the forest and they seemed content to tell us anything we wanted to know, using their hands and their faces in the shared language of food and survival.

As well as the crocodile, which could be killed with care and a good ball from a musket, there was another river beast, like a freshwater whale or seal, something between the two, shy and good to eat. The river teemed with fish and we made nets with which to haul them into our long-boat. We ate all kinds of animals from the forest, the strangeness of them disappearing with their skins. Most of them had a pleasant enough flavour. Some were like great rats and were quite a delicacy. The fruits could have grown in Paradise, they were so bright in colour. Some were of an unbelievable sweetness and others were so sour as to shrivel the gums from our teeth and screw up our faces. If it had not been for the rains, this place might indeed have been Paradise, and there were days when I thought the Black Cook had not simply chosen badly out of his own unacknowledged despair.

We had axes and saws in the ship and the work parties were organized. Those that would not work were reported by Hanno and were flogged by Hasdrubal. The rebellious were hanged. Sometimes I wondered if they all might join together and overthrow the regime of Scipio Africanus, but they were split into too many groups and factions and languages. I began to realize that Hanno had, in fact, separated them into parties largely defined by language or dialect. It

101

was an empire. In their suffering, they had been one people. I still see them as such, but here they were already breaking up into their separate nations. I don't know if the Black Cook saw this.

Those that didn't axe or saw through the great trees, fixed ropes around the trunks and pulled as the clefts began to weaken them; or made up hunting parties; or lit fires; or began work on the shelters that would accommodate us when we moved from the ship to dry land. They were primitive huts, the construction of which came easily to them.

We would work from early morning into the evening when the dark would fall upon us suddenly and we would make our way, first back to the ship and later back to the ramshackle collection of shelters that were now springing up everywhere. There was no pattern to them. If the Black Cook had pictured the city, he had not pictured the stages of transition. Because he could not see them, he could not make anybody else see them and we were lost. His eye would twitch as if he were trying to shift the whole scene into its imagined future, but it kept slipping back. Some days, he would order all the hovels to be pulled down. When it came to it, only one or two would go at any one time, but he would start into the work himself, wrecking homes with all the energy of a natural phenomenon: an earthquake, a great wind or a volcano. He was regarded as such by the Carthaginians, who would build again beneath his watchful eye, only to find him clapping them on the back and telling them that they had built well and he would need good builders.

Alice, whose back was still not healed, busied herself with the building of the house she would live in with Mary and me, much after the fashion of our life together in our cabin on the ship. She built it away from the other shelters, on the edge of the settlement. She had no fear of the forest and at night, after I had made such use of them as I might want to make after a long and weary day's labour, my bones stiff with damp, she would click her tongue over stories of the animals in the forest for Mary, who would laugh, or open her eyes wide in amazement. As she spoke in her low singsong, she would occasionally look towards me to see whether my exclusion was making me angry, as it sometimes did. At these times, she would come to me and soothe my aching limbs with her careful manipulations, jabbering away all the time, but making it sound like a kind of music that she was playing just for me, smoothing my temples and kissing my brow between the notes and I couldn't be angry for long, even though I knew that the story continued and that I could not share it. I would fall asleep under her ministrations.

Alice and Mary learnt words with which they could communicate with me. They would work together, shouting out English words, pointing at different objects as a game. The objects would not always correspond with the words, but that didn't seem to bother them. Gradually the words seemed to build into phrases and I taught them as well as I could, but I never penetrated their language, which was like a secret heart.

The house was round with a diameter of approximately ten feet. In the centre, the roof was around six feet high, running down to maybe four feet high by the walls. Thatched with thick leaves tied into a woven framework of sticks and creepers, it was well made, by which I mean that at least our nights were dry. Even when she was working on other things, Alice would always find time to attend to the constant repairs that were involved in keeping the rain out. She was like a bird in spring, always with her eye open for a scrap of something that might be useful in her endless constructions.

In his gleaming visions, the Black Cook saw the rounded hill and the surrounding plains cleared down to the edges

103

of the sea and the fair fields glistening in the sun as we looked from our city down to the ocean. In calmer moments, pragmatism dictated that we only clear to the landward side of the hill. At this stage, he didn't want to trumpet our appearance too loudly. From the sea, we remained hidden, but even so, the clearances were a monumental task. The trees were so tall and strong, many of the Carthaginians simply strung their shelters out from the sides of the fallen timber.

Many of them died. If it hadn't been for runaways and captives, our numbers would have declined rapidly.

Fever was always there. I took a bad turn with it myself and only survived due to the diligent nursing of Alice and Mary, to whom the Black Cook granted leave of all other work until I was cured.

Alice had a way with medicines and though the plants were new to her, she concocted a mixture of leaves which she ground into a paste and then burnt, filling our shelter with a cleansing smoke. I coughed furiously and she indicated that this was good; that it was the medicine doing its work. When I shivered, Mary would wrap herself round me, kissing the sweat off my brow. I cried out in images, jumbling the burning in the port of G— with the bodies of all those sailors floating in our wake. Bodies burned in the ocean and men screamed with poisonous fire. I was a little boy again, falling out of a tree and Mary was there to catch me and then she wasn't and she was my own Mary and this Mary and all of it was burning or poisoned or drowned and I was falling towards the ocean with my eyes shut tight and wide open at the same time and I was swimming in circles of my own perspiration. There was a figure wrapped around me, from whom I couldn't break free, from whose face I tried in vain to turn away and sometimes it was the Black Cook and sometimes it was Half-Done Dan and he was pulling me down to the bottom of the sea, whoever it was, and then I would see that it was Mary, this Mary and I was swimming up through her trying to reach the surface where I would be able to breathe. She smiled as I swam through her, as if I were a little boy and I was a little boy and an old man at the same time, the one swimming desperately with his eyes shut and the other, whose limbs were like lead, barely able to move for aching in the depths of his bones and his eyes wide open, the fish staring at the strangeness of him.

The words poured out of my fever too fast for Alice or Mary, but as they sat either side of me, squatting on the bare earth of our shelter, they would try to pick out the repeated sounds of some. These, they would answer me back with, closing my lips with a finger and supplying the words taken at random from my babblings, in the hope that they would ease me. And the song, they would stroke my head and sing to me, as a lullaby, the song they had rescued from my wild singing:

Oooissa jolly-butcher-boy
Iss name it a John Bone.
Pray-ay-ay-ay jolly-butcher-boy
Ai ai John Bone alone?
Woe, why shood-a-nee?
Oh, why shood-a-nee?
Come done fa-la wife
Whenee quick with a knife
Ha ha the lady a-gone,
Fa la! Fa la!
Fa tirry fa la!
Ha where hava lady gone gone?

When I was at my most restless, they would sing it together, over and over again, a piece of nonsense. Later, they would sing it to their children, my children, over and over again, as the screams subsided into a heave of the body, the mouth clasped about the nipple, sucking, and the heave subsided into sleep, the mouth still clasped and every now and then sucking like a dog running in its dreams, and then falling back from the breast, the eyes closed and Alice or Mary singing softly, over and over again until they too slept. But that was later.

As I came out of the depths of the fever and seemed to be recovering, Mary would bring me soups that she had made, carefully removing the bones from the fish or fowl or small animal and cutting things up so that I could swallow without making an effort and she would hold my head as she lifted the bowl to my lips. The Black Cook would visit me each day to check on my progress:

'We will soon have you up and about, William. There is much to do. Build yourself up. I don't know why it is that you have two women to look after you, when I have only one. Fate is a strange bedfellow, William. Perhaps, in your case, a whole bevy of bedfellows. Ha! You mustn't let them tire you out. If I come in here and catch you enjoying a bit of pokey-pokey, we'll have you straight back to work. Ha! Ha!'

I tried to laugh with him, but I was still too weak. He clapped me on the shoulder, as my cheeks quivered into half a smile, and left. I was comforted by the concern that the great man showed, but maybe he was as frightened as I would be at the prospect of being left alone with these African-Carthaginians. The strain of forging this people into an empire was telling on him and it was this that served to pull us closer together. I was happy for it.

As I began to sit up, Mary would bring me my fiddle and urge me to play tunes. I would play her a few jigs, half-time, and she would clap along with them, urging me to lift the speed. As often as not, I wouldn't be able to finish. My mind was confused and I would falter. She would smile

106

encouragement and take the instrument from my hands. It was all out of tune and I didn't have the energy to tune it. It was painful listening to it, but I didn't want to disappoint her. She would put it away and bring it back, when she thought I might be up to trying again. It was music that she liked about me. The rest, she didn't know, but took on trust, listening to the music. If musicians were as good as their music, the world would be a fine place, but we're not and it isn't. If I had my fiddle now, I could prove it, playing a sweet lament and in the next moment crushing the life from an innocent animal without the slightest pause, except, perhaps, to put down the bow and pick up a stick. I worried that the tunes would never come back to me; that my ear had been changed by the fever; that I would die, at last, unloved.

Between them, Alice and Mary would help me to the door of the shelter and sit me outside in the sun. They would lean me back gently, against the frame of the door, so that I could see the work going on: the road being cleared down to the river; the stripping of branches and leaves; the binding of tree trunks together in a great raft. In their work-gangs, they laboured continuously, Hanno running between them, as always, passing out orders and moving to the next group. They were like a colony of ants. I felt distant from them. They were a product of my fever. I wiped the sweat from around my eyes, but they were still there.

Alice and Mary started to work, again, on jobs such as branch stripping that could be done close enough to keep an eye on me. Alice had made me a hat. She had woven it out of leaves and grasses. I sat in the sun, wearing my hat of leaves and grasses, watching the ants of a nearby colony and the work of slaves liberated into another slavery that resembled that of ants. If they could have recognized their common suffering, surely they would rebel. Why do ants work so diligently and for so little? What secret did the

Black Cook hold that kept this enterprise together and did he know it? The questions drifted in and out of my mind like the small spiders that moved through my hat of leaves and grass, sometimes spinning down in front of my eyes from the flowers Alice had woven into the brim, their sweet scent light against the heavy richness of the forest after rain, visible clouds lifting about us.

I would sleep to be woken by Alice or Mary bringing me some small morsel of food. Why did they care for me in this way? It was more than duty. There was a kind of love in it, if not for me, for the idea of me. Is there such a thing? If Mary was drawn to my music, this in itself could not be enough. Alice was filled with her own music. Sitting against the door frame of our home, having spent two weeks inside it, sweating so that the smell permeated the walls and now wafted past me in the drying sun so that I could smell the flowers of my hat and the steaming forest and also this third smell, it depended on how I angled my nose, I had begun to think of it as a home and not merely a shelter, I was determined that these things signified a kind of love. It could not have been a love. We did not understand each other and there has never been anything in the least bit lovable about me. Mary, my own Mary, the pig-keeper's daughter, told me stories about love. Once, there was a prince who fell in love with a sleeping princess, her ruby red lips closed and not a word. I wondered how he had known that he loved her. Perhaps she talked in her sleep. It was the kind of fever that lasted a hundred years and he had fallen in love with a voice, whispering, babbling, screaming from the depths of an unfettered imagination, the words having spoken to him of all that was trapped within her sleeping body. Had Mary and Alice fallen in love with a person speaking in his dreams in a language that gave them only random words? Mary had never welcomed my body, or if she had welcomed it, she had made it seem like duty, lifting herself and falling. Alice had always made me lie on my back, hers still painful from the flogging, and later it became custom with us and as I lay there, she would continue her conversation with Mary or the air, as if I wasn't really there at all. Can habit grow into love without ever passing through understanding?

Sitting against the door frame of our home, my home and Alice's home and Mary's home, wearing the hat Alice had woven from leaves and grasses, smelling the flowers fixed into the brim and my own sweat and the steaming forest, watching the spider that spun its line of web down towards my chest and holding myself very still so that it would not be deflected from its paths, I decided that it was love for the idea of me. I had been cut off from my people even more cruelly than they had, I reasoned in self-pity. Here we were in the middle of a wild forest. Africa was forest. This was not their forest, but it was close enough as to make no difference. This was a good home for them and that is why they were content to work. The Black Cook had chosen well for both them and for himself. This was the image he carried in his head of home, through all the years when it had not been home. He remembered the forest, I thought. I remembered individual trees in a flat landscape. I could climb the trees of this unfamiliar continent and see nothing but the unfamiliar. This might as well have been Africa to me, for all the comfort it brought. I sat in the sun, watching the working gangs; watching Hanno running between them; watching the Black Cook busy with his plans; watching Mary and Alice stripping branches from tree trunks and every now and then looking up to see that I was all right and I would smile faintly to let them know that I was all right, but still not strong, and I thought all this. I thought that their love cherished an idea of abandonment. I had become a totem of loss for them and they cared for me as they might care for a wounded animal, because it made

109

them feel strong to see something more pitiful than they were. They had grown in strength and stature in this new land, whereas I had been laid low.

When Mary approached me with a bright yellow fruit she had discovered in the branches of the tree she and Alice had been at work on, I spat it out. I stood up so that I could turn away from her, turn back in towards the fetid smells of the shelter, and I could hear Alice laugh as I fell over.

FIFTEEN

The rats are not impressed.

'That was very slow,' I am told. 'Why does this clearing in the forest merit so much detail?' they ask.

I answer: because it is a strange country.

'It is all a strange country.'

And then another voice: 'Why do you not tell us more of these Great Rats who were such a delicacy?'

SIXTEEN

The Black Cook had wanted me in good health, body and mind, for a piece of monumental insanity.

'Leave her there and the worms will eat her until she sinks down into the mud for wreckage and driftwood.'

'It's madness.'

'Or one of these bastards will get the idea of sailing back to Africa. They'll not get out of the river without running her aground and I'll have to hang half of them. It will be harder work, then, with fewer hands.'

It was hard to argue with this relaxed and jovial pragmatism. 'But we'll have no means of escape,' I tried.

'There is no way back and there is no other way forward, Will.'

'We could take her apart and rebuild her on site.'

'Do you have the skill?'

I didn't. If I was shaking my head, I was not saying no, but shaking it in wonder at the very idea, its impossibility and the pointlessly proposed exertion of all our efforts on its behalf.

'Do you want them to say of us: they lived in the trees like the animals of the forest? Should they say: they were runaways, who scratched a life like savages? Are they to see New Carthage or just note, in passing, a rough clearing and a few huts thatched with leaves? History is an effort of the

will. When they see a ship, sailing on the crest of a continent, they will ask: what race of men can have done this?
It will be a sign of greatness. The forests of the Earth are
not impenetrable, for we sail above them. They are like the
sea to us: there to be crossed and conquered.'

'The river is more than three miles away.'

He was resolved, however, lucid and convincing. I saw it
and I fell in love with the idea of it. I did not understand
it, but I was still suffering from a touch of fever. This was
the purpose of the great raft I had seen under construction.
We were to take the keel off the ship and haul her on to the
raft, which by then would have axles and great wheels cut
from the largest of the tree trunks, and on this she would
be pulled up the cleared road from the river, to the summit
of the hill that formed New Carthage. I was needed for some
of the mechanical aspects of the task. He had been waiting
for my recovery. He would take charge of the hauliers, but
he needed someone, who knew ships, to stay with the ship.
This is what he told me, but as I considered the matter, I
thought he might also feel concern at the great possibility
of rebellion. He wanted his gangs well supervised. Then
again, as I thought the matter over, I realized, most of all,
he wanted the achievement recorded for posterity. I have
done my best.

It was certainly a source of wonder. When we had the
ship out of the water, Indians began to appear at the edge
of the clearings. As we began to haul the thing on its long
journey against gravity, more gathered, witnesses to an
acknowledged marvel. After a few days of watching, they
began to join us on the ropes and help. The languages of
three continents combined to curse and cheer, groan and
then laugh. I began to learn the importance of not understanding. I am still trying to reach that state of wonder.

There was no rebellion. Three of the Indians died when
the ship rolled back a quarter of a mile, to rest again in the

mud of the river, but their companions didn't desert us. Five of the Carthaginians died at the same time, two crushed with the Indians and three more, who died as a result of the injuries they sustained. There were complaints. There was screaming and shouting; jabberings at high speed and high volume, incomprehensible and wild, directed at everybody but the author of their sufferings.

It was three days before we got back to where we had been, but a day of that was taken up making her secure on the raft again, and in making repairs. When she was ready to begin the ascent again, the Indians appeared with flowers from the forest, which they used to decorate the ropes and spars. When he closed his eye, the Black Cook had not seen flowers.

'Did I order this?' He shook the rigging to dislodge an Indian, who was climbing towards the spars of the main mast. The Indian looked at him in innocent surprise from the deck. Scipio Africanus was still shaking the rigging, even though the Indian was no longer there. He was shaking from the inside. Details affected him far more than the greater movements they were a part of. Dido took a flowered creeper from the Indian's hand. She removed the Black Cook's three-cornered hat and wound the flower round it, before she replaced it on his head.

'Give me flowers,' she said to the other Indians, who had gathered at the incident. They understood her gestures. She took up the fallen Indian's work.

What the Indians and Dido began, the Carthaginians continued and each night, as the ship was wedged and staked into its resting place, flowers, fruits and leafy creepers would be added until it became a thing of fantasy.

'People need such fantastic things,' said the Black Cook, days later.

'I don't understand it,' I said.

'If you understood, it would not be fantastic. People do

114

not understand empires, for example, but rather, marvel at their audacity. The empire that is understood, is diminished. If people think about what they are doing, they shrink from its absurdity. I give them pictures beyond understanding.'

He sat to the side, watching the work of the evening, as a hundred hands wove the forest into the beached ship, taking possession of their collective labour. The slip-back had been caused by exhaustion. A rope had snapped and the extra strain suddenly exerted on the other ropes had led first one and then all the gangs to lose control of it in the mud. As dispensation, the work on hauling, from then on, only lasted five hours in any day, so that it became a kind of holiday, or festival. Meals were cooked from the supplies of the ship, which had been carried up to our encampments separately. If there was a pattern to things, it would rain during the night and into the mornings, but from noon, it would begin to dry. We would begin the haulage during the rain, usually, and things would improve, so that by the time the day's labours were finished, the mood would relax.

'I give them pictures. See, they embellish them.'

SEVENTEEN

ALICE'S STORY OF THE GREAT BOAT

It is one thing to sail a great boat over the ocean, but it is another thing to sail up the sides of a mountain. See the ship where it sails: where it had sheets of cloth with which it could catch the wind, now it has flowers with which it can capture the insects of the forest. Have you seen the ant? How it can carry a leaf along the ant road, though the leaf is ten times the size of an ant? With the sweet-scented flowers of the forest, we captured the strength of a million insects so that this ship became lighter with the nectar of each blossom: with the juice of each fruit dripping from these vines on to the dried wooden deck of it. The great boat itself can taste the rich juices. They remind it of the time when it too was forest, before men came to cut down the trees that were carved into its planks and masts. The grain of the wood opens up a thousand mouths to taste this memory and draw strength from it, for the memory is as sweet as the fruit itself and as sweet as the nectar of the flowers and the smell of the leaves in the sunshine that follows rain. Each ship knows that, truly, it belongs in the heart of the forest and that the ocean is an exile from its own heart. The grains of its timbers open in a thousand eyes and it

116

sees the brightly coloured birds swim through the air. It knows that it has returned. We return with it, slowly, inch by inch, making our way to the home that Two-World Dan found for us at the top of a hill, that is the bottom of an ocean. When we need him, he will dive into that ocean, and, swimming, he will walk out of the forest and find the ship, which he sees as a shape on the waves.

The audience of lost souls that had first gathered at Alice's feet on board *The Pride of M—*, still gathered whenever she lifted her voice into a story. Alice was a prophet for them. They became known as the Dans, revering her for her relationship with the saviour she had promised. She laughed at them, but they took this just as a prophet's strange ways. Her status grew with each story. Across all the language groups of the Carthaginians she was respected and even Hanno was half in her sway. He translated all but the last part for us.

The Black Cook was intrigued by Alice, not least because he didn't understand what it was that she was peddling in this open market of narrative. He would create a story of bold actions and find it had come back changed beyond recognition. He was caught between the old desire to subjugate, that had sustained him until now, and a new-found pleasure, inspiring the unpredictable. It was an uneasy pleasure. If Hanno had translated the part that Two-World Dan played, Alice would have hanged. There were many, many stories. If I could remember them now, all of them, I would be able to retell the whole story from start to finish, not my story, but hers. Even in this imprisonment with the flesh falling away from my bones and my hair still growing and my nails still growing, I would be content, listening to her with those parts of me that were still alive though my mind was dead and my heart had stopped beating, because it was a story that didn't need me.

The Black Cook knew that Alice did not fit into his vast scheme and the fact that she set in path other patterns disturbed him. If he had not predicted the help offered by the Indians, he had felt certain of the compliance of the Carthaginians. The force of his own will would hold them together on an epic journey across mountains, for this was his version of the crossing of the Alps. The ship was his heroic impossibility. It was an army of war elephants. The breathtaking imagination of the move would defeat his enemies in their souls, where the fiercest battles are fought between empires. The Carthaginians would haul the ship where he told them, because he was their Hannibal; their great general. He would quash all talk of mutiny because his greatness promised greatness. But he wanted the story fixed.

Like all of us, he was a little afraid of Alice. If Hanno didn't translate some parts of the stories, the Black Cook knew it and preferred it that way. My status grew within the community as a result of Alice's concern for my health; her willingness to remain with me; her visible love.

After another two days we reached the top of the first slope, the slope leading up from the river, and had a day hauling the ship over level ground before we came to the slope of New Carthage itself. It could have been done more quickly. Although it was hard work, once we were embarked on it, helped by the Indians and all of us committed to the task, we could have moved at twice the speed, but I was at all times concerned for the stresses we were placing on the structure. A ship is not designed for hills and I was worried that it would somehow pull itself apart. I am not a naval engineer. I became attached to her, seeing her in her slow climb along this broad dirt track, whose seagulls were parrots and other exotic birds. The portage of ships between seas or between lakes was something I knew of, although I had never witnessed one. The fact that ours said goodbye for ever to the waters of the world, to my mind, placed a greater strain on the structural integrity of the ship. The vessel might break up out of despair, I thought, but I shared these thoughts with no one. I adopted Alice's interpretation: a ship's joy at being amongst trees again. Sometimes, as I watched her move, I could believe it and I was filled with joy myself in her great celebration, but I insisted on regular halts so that I could check the timbers inside and out.

In fact, a ship, being built to withstand the strains of unpredictable seas, great hollows that open up beneath her and vast batterings against her sides, has little difficulty with the regulated strain of ropes and the bumps of a dirt track. The journey was not a humiliation for her. She achieved a majesty in her progress, decked in wild flowers, her sails furled. I could have stood and watched. I would have been happier, in some ways, on the ropes with Alice and Mary and the others. When she had slipped back, I had been told to examine her carefully for any damage, though, and this had become my main task. This was what was important. There was no real need for more than one in the supervision of the labour, any more. People developed a rhythm to the work, responding quickly to any sudden order, and I became a naval engineer.

If the ship was able to withstand the strains of the journey, was I? And have I ever recovered? The Carthaginians and the Indians knew nothing of ships. They would not have given thought to the possibility that the ship might break up, if it hadn't been for the diligence of my examinations. I would stand at her prow, leaning out over the bowsprit, and shout to the Black Cook that all was well. There would be a great cheer and the haulage teams would take up their ropes again and pull. The examinations themselves developed a kind of rhythm and the day's journey would break into a pattern of pauses: the haulage itself

119

would break down into haul and rest and haul and rest and then, after an hour or so I would cry 'Wait!' and there would be a rest for ten minutes or so, while I carried out an inspection. Once a day, there would be a longer inspection.

It was a task that earned me respect, for the health of this great thing, which had become the shared concern and happiness of all of us, was in my hands. I was not idle during the periods of haulage, either. I would run about the ship making things secure; making minor adjustments. I would climb down the side, while she was moving, and walk about her. Sometimes I would call 'Wait!' from the ground, as if I had seen something that worried me, that no one else had noticed; could have noticed. Out of the corner of my eye, I would try to find Alice or Mary and in their response I would assess my performances. My gestures and expressions took on a theatrical turn as each day I tried to grow in their estimation, recovering ground lost during my illness.

'No! Wait a while! Wait! Have the crossbeams shifted in their axis? Surely not! Ten minutes, I beg of you, ten minutes, while I check the crossbeams for their alignments.'

It was not that this was understood in any respect, but I would stretch my arms and act out the ship's obvious distress so that they knew the technical credentials of a particular stoppage. The Black Cook was cheered considerably by my pantomimes. Some days he couldn't get enough.

'Take a line on the mizzen from that bowsprit, William. Are we true?' he would call out.

'Strike me down if she hasn't moved a couple of inches out, Scipio. Haul more on the left! On the left! We must equalize the tensions or she's lost!'

'Haul more on the left!' the Black Cook would shout, indicating the gangs on the left side and acting out the great force required. Hanno would translate, keen to demonstrate his own function, but I had the better of him in those days and he knew it.

120

I thought of Half-Done Dan: 'A captain is like an extra bollock.' I missed his unreserved gloom and despondency. My performances were exhausting. My mind was being pulled in such contradictory directions. It had not been built to sustain unpredictable forces. I wanted to rip the foliage from the rigging and scream out: 'No! She will founder! Our dreams will be driftwood in a green sea!' At the same time I wanted all of them, each in their own language, to look up at me, standing at the ship's prow, and exclaim: 'He is the Pride of New Carthage! He is the Flower of the Forest!' For all my inspections, I could see nothing that I could interpret one way or another, so that if I did order them to haul more on the left, I would suddenly panic and order them to put their shoulders to the right. One minute I was convinced of disaster, the next I would believe again. Alice would look and I was convinced she saw straight through me. Mary would look at me and her eyes would be wide. But then, did I catch Alice opening her eyes wide in amazement? And did Mary narrow hers in suspicion? I wanted them both to open their eyes wide in amazement. I wanted them both to narrow their eyes in suspicion. Were they doing neither? I wanted to keep my eyes open and I wanted to shut them fast. I wanted to shout out in triumph and I wanted to fall from the bowsprit to be crushed beneath the wheels of sawn tree trunks. I wanted to jump and land on Mary and Alice, who would turn from their labours and cushion me in their softness and we would all be crushed beneath the rolling ship and that would be an end to it.

Alice was singing her stories and Mary was listening. Alice was telling a story of how I sat in the prow of the great ship, the bowsprit between my legs, or maybe she was singing another story and I was not a part of the risings and fallings of her voice as she rode upon me, Mary hanging on every word, and I was hanging on to driftwood in an open

121

sea, a great ship having vanished beneath me in the storm. I wanted them as my empire, but I was falling under the sway of theirs. This was not an empire. There are no captains in a wreckage. I will be captain, I cry, barely able to keep afloat, an extra bollock and a bollock short of what was required.

The next day would begin the ascent of the slopes of New Carthage itself. I was falling in love with two women and all we could share of understanding was: William, Mary, Alice, Eat, Drink, Yes, No, Good, Bad, Here, There, Forest, River, Tree, Ship, Flower, Fish, Bird, Cat, Pig, Rat, Dog, Deer, Monkey, Sun, Cloud, Mist, Rain, Home, Hair, Eyes, Nose, Ears, Mouth, Lips, Arms, Hands, Fingers, Titties, Belly, Belly button, Buttocks or Arse, Foot, Toe, Ankle, Leg, Thigh, Poke-Hole, Glory-Hole, Honey-Pot or Cunt, Poker, Prick, Dick, Parson or Preacher, Pokey or Bumbo.

Was it enough? I had experienced the pangs of love before. Thinking of my own Mary, when I was far out at sea, but that was different because it was an absence; the odd girl or woman, paid for by the Black Cook, who had shown some tenderness and whose arms I didn't want to leave when we were sailing that morning, but they were soon forgotten. I had never before spent more than two nights in the company of a woman. It was not that I had ever said that much to women since I had gone to sea, but the sense that I could have done if I had wanted to. I would redouble my efforts at their education, I decided. I would make them understand me. Alice would sing her stories in a language we would share. I would tell them my stories and Mary would listen in the same way she listened to Alice. We would cut down on bumbo and have lessons every night. I was determined. Love brings its responsibilities.

EIGHTEEN

She began to move up the slopes of the city, itself, between its great, white-walled mansions, along its broad avenues. I sat athwart the bowsprit looking down on the straining bodies of Mary and Alice and I felt my heart fill with love, the rain falling on their backs and their bare feet slipping in the mud of the dirt track and the rain falling across my face, dripping from my nose and soaking through my shirt to a goose-pimpled body they loved not as an idea, but in our own kingdom, carved from the privations of this world. I, who was not an emperor, could be content with a kingdom.

'Wait!' I cried, just so that they would turn round, when the wedges had been fixed beneath the wheels and they could relax. Then I would shout: 'Rest!' and I would see their faces with the rain streaming down them, their eyes screwed up against it, their hands on their foreheads to shield their eyes and the rain dripping from their chins. I would give a quick smile, before I ran off about my work, that was no work at all, but a justification for stopping them. In my love, at times, it was as if only Mary and Alice were hauling the ship: just the two of them, one on the left and one on the right, although, in reality, they both hauled on the right-hand side, but closing my eyes, with my legs swinging on either side of the bowsprit, they were pulling me, each with one rope over their shoulders, and I wanted to cry out: 'She's moving! Take me to the top of the hill!' I imagined all the others standing at the side, watching and cheering as Alice and Mary pulled the ship and pulled me, because suddenly in my imagination I was as large as the ship between my legs, like a child with a toy.

Where are you now, Alice? And Mary, where have you gone? You were my own Mary more than my own Mary. You were like giants of the sea, the ropes cutting into your shoulders and the water rolling down your backs, as if you had risen from the waves.

In a day and a half we had reached the summit. As we approached it, they had risen to the occasion and I had left off my performance. There had been a couple of other deaths over the whole journey: one Indian and one Carthaginian. In different incidents, they had both died when the wheels they were pushing had broken. We had prepared a number of wheels in readiness, however, and they were soon replaced. Barca had a leg broken in a similar incident. It healed crooked and he had a lopsided walk when he was able to walk again. When we reached the top, there was a great cheer, such as I had never heard before from any crowd. We made her fast, anchoring her with ropes to stakes driven into the ground and to the trees that stood behind her. When she was secure we just stood back laughing and clapping each other on the back. I stood with my arms round Alice and Mary, my left hand feeling the smoothness of Mary's back and my right hand feeling the ridges across Alice's back. It was honest contentment.

Alice collected flowers. In our hut I lay with Mary. I was filled with the energy of our achievement, and Mary smiled between the soft kisses she offered my lips and my neck. Love mingled with sweat as we laboured about each other and I tried to find words she understood that would give expression to my joy.

124

'Wait, William Bone,' she said.

It was a new word. She had learnt it in the public arena and now she applied it to these intimacies: it was beyond the best of my hopes and I could not contain my excitement. As we separated, Alice appeared in the doorway with her flowers. We dressed and she decorated our clothes with flowers as we stood for her. She decorated herself and laughed at the way I kept looking at them both, first her and then Mary and then back at her. She had made garlands for our heads and we made our way up the hill like May Day revellers and I was the King with two Queens and the ship was our Maypole.

Adapting their forest knowledge, the Carthaginians had begun to make a kind of palm wine. They had prepared large quantities of it for the day when we would reach the top of the hill. Hollowed-out gourds were passed around and we drank. The alcohol gave rise to another burst of activity. If the ship had been decorated on its journey, this was nothing on the work that now began, with all the energy of their release from labour and all the wild confidence of palm wine. Flowers and vines and great palm fronds were twisted into every inch of rigging and along every foot of timber. Swarming over her, they created a vast anarchic beauty. I was worried for the safety of the ship, but nothing could have prevented them. They had taken her from the sea that they had feared, and they had made her their own. Now they were threading her into the surrounding forest. Her timbers would take root and she would grow with them at the heart of their city.

They held on to ropes and laughed. They drank great scoops of palm wine and lay on the decks staring up through the joy of their creation.

The Black Cook didn't drink. The forest lay at his feet, a kind of Italy, and he didn't know what to do with it. In his head, he saw Hannibal crossing and recrossing this vast green land in search of Rome, but Rome lay in his heart and he could not see it. No. He was here. Being here, he had defeated his enemies. Could they have done this? He would wait. There would be a sign and he would know what to do. He stood gazing out from the celebrations, searching for a sign, but there were no signs.

'Love is a kingdom,' I said. 'Let us call it S—. We sail into her harbour at T—. I have been crossing her mountain ranges in search of U—.'

He didn't answer.

'Not you, but U—, you understand. Love is such a little kingdom. Do you think?'

He thought nothing.

'I'm in love, you know,' I said. 'I think I love them. I want them to have my child,' I managed, lifting my head from my drink to see that he was no longer there.

Mary and Alice found me and I told them: 'I love you and I want you to have my child.' They laughed at the slur of my words. 'More lessons tomorrow,' I said and they hoisted me up between them, dragging me off to a dance that was taking place between the ship and the forest on the other side. I can remember no more of that night. I woke up on the deck of the ship. Mary and Alice were lying a few feet away. Lessons were out of the question. I hauled myself over, so that I could lie between them.

The Black Cook declared a public holiday throughout his domains.

NINETEEN

The gaoler speaks.

Out of all the days when he could have spoken, or the gaoler before him could have spoken, or the gaoler before him but one, or any of the others over all of the years, today he opens his mouth and words come out.

The cell has been on fire, today, with a fierce light. I couldn't put pen to paper for the interwoven colours flaming across its surface. I was walking sideways around the cell, pressing my hands against the burning walls, trying to push through and out. The door opened and I ignored it. Who can eat when the world is on fire? Who would drink when the tongue is a single flame? I continued my examination of the visible world and gave him my back.

Major James Tulliver, tired of waiting, has sent him to finish me off. A sudden blow of an axe. A pistol shot to the head. Or Major James Tulliver has sailed away; sailed away years ago. The new man, we discover, has no interest in literary patronage. I suddenly feel my hair pulled roughly back and the poison burning between my lips, trickling into my mouth wrenched open and I have to swallow. None of these things, however. The words open a path through the flames and I turn around.

'What?' I ask, staring at him as the after-effect of the sound echoes in my ears. 'What did you say?' I know he has spoken, but my mind has been elsewhere. I haven't been expecting it. The sound of it has lost all sense. I heard it but I am not able to interpret. The cell is grey again. Even the light from the window is grey. His voice must have an extinguishing quality. We stand with an extraordinary silence between us. My own questions don't seem to penetrate it.

'Please. I'm sorry. You must forgive me. I was otherwise engaged. I didn't hear. Well, I heard, but, I'm sorry. You understand, it has been many years and I haven't heard any voice but my own.'

A cock crows and a rat pokes his head from a hole in the corner of the steps. His whiskers twitch and he washes his forefeet with a deliberate tongue. I stare at him and then, in a sudden panic, back at the gaoler, afraid I might lose this moment.

'Words count for nothing,' says the rat, looking up from his ablutions. 'They're gone as soon as said. Only meat is eternal.' The cell is alive with silent accusation and a thousand eyes and the rat is cleaning his tail. 'Meat walks on a thousand legs,' he says. 'Words evaporate like the soul between teeth.'

'Many years.' I concentrate on the gaoler as hard as I can. 'No words but my own. What was it you said?'

I can make out each word. I can feel my lips open and close and my tongue move between my teeth, against my teeth, against the roof of my mouth and down, almost to its own root like a spring. There are sounds, but they do not affect the silence between us, which is physical, as if the air has become solid. I want to open my mouth wide and scream, but think better of it. He has spoken to me and he might still speak again. It is a possibility. When no one will speak to you, it is easy to construct a *modus operandi*. In silence, you draw up the laws that govern a silent world. Hypothesis, over the years, takes on the certainty of cast iron. There is a brittle quality to it, but it is too strong for a man alone to break. The mind needs to be surrounded with some degree of certainty, or it becomes ungovernable. My certainties have been the walls of this cell and its silences.

'They will not speak to you,' I told myself and constructed a measure of sanity upon the empirical evidence for this fixed law. Once in a hundred years and a man speaks: you are left with nothing. What system can take account of events without reason or pattern and gone before you notice they are there, like a fish jumping in a river, was there a flash that caught your eye, but all you see are the circles in the water telling you that you missed it.

The door slams shut again. He never spoke. There is something in the mind that seeks to destroy all its creations. I invented his words and that is why I didn't hear them.

I scream.

I can feel my mouth open wide, tearing at the muscles in my face. I can feel my throat straining, my tongue curved back on itself, but I don't hear the sound. I am not screaming and he did speak to me. The walls are damp and grey and I am an old man edging round my cell and trying to find the signs of fire again, but they have vanished for ever. I am left wading through a palpable stillness, as against the tide.

Something has happened. It is as if time has stopped, but I am still moving, as my fingernails and my hair will move, grow on after the beating of my heart has stopped. I hold up my hand and move it through the silence, but it makes no impact. When I used to move, the air opened up before me and closed behind me, but now I move through it as if it is not there or I am not here or we no longer have any relationship.

'What has happened here?' I know I have asked the question and I can hear it, but I do not feel my lips move.

129

The rats continue their lives as if nothing has happened. They sniff in reflex interest as they pass the shit hole. Their whiskers twitch. They approach the plate of food I have been left and begin to eat at its contents. I watch them without protest. Who could eat at a time like this, when even time has abandoned us? Here in this cell, if I have on occasions lost track of time, at least I always knew that it was passing. Words and now this.

Everything is the same, but something has happened. The rats go about their rat lives, their feet scratching and scrabbling at the edges of the silence, but they do not speak to me any more. In my pain I denied them and now they have left me. Perhaps they were testing me. The gaoler's words were an act of ventriloquism.

I was caught off-guard and now I am alone. If I could add up the days and say, 'On Tuesday, 9th July, 17—, the seven thousandth day of his imprisonment, these things happened: a door opened; a gaoler spoke; a door closed; in the silence even the rats stopped speaking and time stopped,' I would say it, but there are no certainties any more. I have been caught off-guard and everything has crumbled except the walls that circumscribe the visible world. I have crumbled, or am crumbling, like an emperor bereft of empire, like the Black Cook, like a king without a kingdom.

I am alone and this cell is the absence of love, which was a country I could have travelled through all my life, like the king who abandons his crown and takes on the clothes of a simple man; who takes a stick and walks from village to village seeking forgiveness from people who no longer recognize him. A small country, but a lifetime of penitence.

Every stone in the floor of this cell is a village where I am no longer recognized, but neither do I recognize each village and I am asking forgiveness of those I can neither see, nor hear, nor smell, nor touch, nor understand.

I say that these things happened today, because the present tense sucks in my words like a vacuum, but I do not mean happened and I do not mean today and the rats are right. I am writing this down and each word takes a year to write in a cell where time has come to a halt.

Today is a bad day.

TWENTY

The fields of New Carthage, burnt and cut and dug from the flat land below the slopes of the city, are a miserable affair. The rains tear at our loose soil and drive gullies through it. The Black Cook is no farmer. He has brought seed with him, secreted in the ship's stores.

'Fields of wheat, William,' he says as they are planted.

We are grateful to the Indians, who teach us about the roots of the forest and all the things that can feed the stomach in a land of plenty. A man might die of starvation and not know the food that surrounds him.

'They must be brought under our will,' says the Black Cook.

I counsel restraint. 'They are a friendly nation.'

'Will you live on dirt and lizards for the rest of your days?'

'How will a military action change our lives?' I ask. Love gives me confidence.

'Every action changes everything. I have introduced reason to the forest. It must either flourish or die.'

He lives on board the ship now, *The Pride of M——*. She is his palace. He lives in her with Dido, who moves about the decks and cabins with a quiet diligence, constantly renewing the flowers and the vines from a stock that is brought daily to the ship's side. He has moved back to the galley. The failure of the crop has hit him hard.

'I have voices in my head,' he says. 'Two voices and both of them generals: where are their strategies, William?'

I have never seen him so low.

'There are your own strategies,' I suggest. 'You brought us here.'

'I am not a military man.'

I am writing this in the silence that continues to fall like rain. It is all happening so long ago but in front of my eyes and the narrative surrounds me. I see the rats but they pay me no attention. There is a lightness in my head. I see them through the history conjured between us, but their mouths are shut.

He stirs his pot, a stew of lizards and roots. This is the heart of his palace.

'They are in your sphere of influence.'

I say these things to comfort him, but he has retreated into himself. He reads from Livy and he cooks. Many of the Indian women have moved to our city and coupled with our citizens. The womenfolk of the ones that died in the portage were the first. Others come. North of here, great disturbances have sent whole populations moving along this coast. Small groups of women come sometimes and stay. They are courted with offers of food. Sometimes, it seems to me, that a great empire could be built out of these dispossessed. Just by raising a standard, they would come, runaways and Indians, and an empire could be built without conquest.

'When the rains have finished,' I suggest. 'That is the time for military campaigns.' We both know that the rains will never finish for long enough.

Never break the peace, for fear that a worse one will come

133

in its place. If I have a philosophy, this is my philosophy and then I think where it has led me. This is not the Black Cook's philosophy and I think where his philosophy has led him. It is as if there is a malign spirit at large in the world, whose work it is to undo philosophy.

'Listen what I have to say. Dido live in this one small village, edge of great empire. Africa. She never see the heart of it. Many small kings many. Many lords many many. One lord he fight one king: goodbye Dido sold for slave. Goodbye: she never see his body, the father of her child. Goodbye: she never see her son. Tears many many. No good. What is great empire? Fat man so fat he no get hisself up out of bed. Foot fall off, that fat man feel nothing at all.'

Dido speaks and I am struck dumb. I search her face for bruises, but see no evidence. The Black Cook fingers his old ladle, but he does nothing. In his eye, he dreams of the greatness of Dido's empire and of trouble in the distant lands of his imagination.

'I will send an expeditionary force,' he says and I am not sure if he is attacking the village of the Indians or saving Dido from the slave traders.

He does not walk among us these days. Sometimes we see him gazing down at us from the deck. He is camped on a hillside, considering a campaign that has lost its way. We are the field of a battle that is being lost in his mind. In the rain, he wears his cloak. When the sun shines, he takes it off. He always wears his three-cornered hat.

I visit him every day to talk over my observations and his; to take instructions; to listen to anything he has to say. Hanno visits him also. He visits in the morning and I visit in the evening. Hanno takes full responsibility for the running of our colony these days. He gives me a wide berth. He despises me, I can see it in his eyes, but he is also a little jealous. I am closer to the Black Cook. He would seize power, if he could be certain of it. He would kill me, but he is afraid of Alice. Sometimes, I think I will kill him, but New Carthage would collapse without him and I would be butchered in the chaos that followed. The runaways always look at me with suspicion. Hanno fears chaos too. This is why he makes no moves. I think back to those days when we lifted a ship from the water and carried her across mountains, an army of disparate tribes.

Survival has such purpose. It is the common sense through which we have fallen apart. The purpose of individuals cannot be held together. I think about Dido's words. The fat man doesn't move from his bed, maybe because he has died. This is why his foot has fallen off. His foot is alive in the way that rotting meat is alive. The heart of the empire is alive in the same way. Empires die long after their emperors and an emperor can die long before he realizes it.

Fat men go to bed, because it has become a strain to walk about. They do not want to think about their limbs. They do not want to think about the folds of flesh that hang from their bodies. None of it is what they planned. In bed, they can stare at the ceiling. Their hearts stop and they are still staring at the ceiling. What do I know about fat men? All of this I have thought from a consideration of Dido's words and I am filled with shame at my own feeble efforts at educating Mary and Alice.

They are both pregnant as a result of my other labours, so, whilst I am filled with shame, I am also pleased with myself. I place my hand on their smooth rounded bellies, tight with my children, and smile in a demonstration of my happiness that leaves the muscles of my face aching. I want to tell them about my worries. I want to say that life here has become dangerous. It is not the fever or the snakes or the crocodiles, but ourselves; that we cannot hold together. This never was an empire. It is an empire within other empires and within it there are other empires struggling back and forth across a continent that is too small.

135

I want to say that there are runaways and Indians moving up and down this coast and some of them stay here and are joined in these struggles, but some of them move on and maybe they find happiness in another place. We could leave, cross our own mountains and find a new city. We could search this land for somewhere, my children in your bellies or in our arms, somewhere there are no other empires. I smile and they smile back so that our faces ache, because I don't know how to say these things.

I make a circle round us. I touch Mary on the head and Alice on the head and my child in Mary's belly and my child in Alice's belly and I say: 'William Bone's family.'

The times when we are happy vanish so quickly, it is difficult to make them solid in the imagination.

'William Bone's happy family,' I say, pointing to my smile and this is another lesson finished for the day. Alice is larger than Mary, because she is at least a month further advanced in her pregnancy. Around the edges of her great belly, I look at the marks of the whip that flicked round her sides gripping her momentarily before it was drawn back for the next stroke. She holds my hand against the scars.

'Why do you tell stories?' I ask her. 'There never has been a story that didn't cause trouble.'

I sit as wide-eyed as Mary, listening to her. There is something in her voice that holds you. It holds all of them. These days, when the Black Cook no longer moves among us, she can be working at preparing food and she will suddenly start telling a story and two or three will gather to listen to it. Sometimes I try to pull her away, but she laughs and brushes me aside. As her belly has grown, she has drawn more and more. People stand and listen to her stories and look at her belly as if that is where the stories come from, because there is something about the rounded belly of a woman advanced in pregnancy that draws the eye. Sometimes, the baby kicks as she tells the story and she laughs and then they all laugh.

136

The baby kicks as Alice tells me this story now and I feel it and she laughs and I laugh, but I stop laughing before she does.

The Dans have taken to carving sticks; to carrying them about wherever they go. They stride across the shambles of this hillside and meet each other, leaning on their sticks and pointing to some far country. Barca, whose leg was crushed, carries a stick, but the Dans' sticks are different. The carvings are rough and carry no meaning for me, but they tell stories. The rain carries stories in this place. Stories run down this hillside and through our pitiful fields and take the soil with them as they move across the landscape searching out the river. It is a fever.

The sticks are made for Two-World Dan and for his return that has been vouchsafed them. This has helped to explain one of the more curious sights, where half a dozen of them gather in an evening. Against the fading light, you can see them leaning on their sticks and shuffling in a one-legged dance. There are too many one-legged men in this world. Hanno has a stick, but it has no carvings. It is a symbol of his office and carries any meaning you care to give it. Alice doesn't have a stick. She has been given many, but she burns them on the fire. The Dans do not understand her, but in this they are not alone. The stories still pour out of her and her belly still grows.

The Black Cook sees none of this. Standing on the deck, he cannot see the carvings on the sticks. If he sees the strange dances he thinks nothing of them. I am at fault for not telling him of these things. Hanno also does not tell him. We are both at fault with different motives. But there is a blindness in the Black Cook these days. When I speak to him, something has gone out of him.

When he speaks to me, I have to work out who it is. Sometimes, he is Hannibal, whose voice is rich and arrogant. Sometimes, he is his namesake, Scipio Africanus

Major, whose voice is like salt. Sometimes, in the two voices, he conducts a debate. It is as if his own voice has expelled these qualities and maybe this is what has gone out of him. When I hear his own voice now, it seems quite empty.

I am standing beside him, looking across the early evening on the hillside at the people going about their lives. Above us, a man in the crows-nest keeps watch for passing ships he can see beyond the tops of the trees; for strangers approaching the city. He has climbed the rigging of flowers and leaves and today he can't see any of these things although he can see for miles because it is not raining. The Black Cook has not been speaking and now he speaks:

'I have a better understanding of the heart's aspirations than of the politic mind.'

The voice is sharp and dull all at the same time. Hanno is standing with a group of Dans. He leans on his stick which is not carved, in the same way that the Dans lean on their carved sticks. An evening conversation. The Dans are of no use to anyone, but Hanno cultivates them.

Today Alice is giving birth to my daughter, Elizabeth, as dark as her mother, and already the singsong voice is telling this child about the world she has entered.

Today Mary is giving birth to my son, Henry, only a few shades lighter than Elizabeth. Mary is holding her belly as the labour begins. She gives me my fiddle. She does not want my help with the birth. She wants me to play music for the child who has not yet arrived. She does not want a slow air, she wants jigs and reels and hornpipes. As Henry's head appears between his mother's legs he hears a hornpipe called *Henry Taylor's* and that is why I call my son Henry. When he cries, I cry on the fiddle, incorporating it into the tune. Mary is too tired to laugh, but Alice laughs.

I want it all to stop. I want to shout: 'Stop!' and see everything finish together, to see it all complete. I say this in my
heart and I am like the fool granted his wish, because you
never get what you mean and I didn't mean this, everything
I have ever known finishing together, the complete works,
the ghosts of every word, of every dream, of every memory
crowding into this narrow cell. I can see it all and touch
none of it. I want none of it. I cannot close my eyes.

TWENTY-ONE

Today the one-legged man has come to New Carthage, Josiah Peabody the preacher. He has ten Indians with him. He has filled them with an understanding of Christ's love and they carry his supplies. They carry him across the river. Singing hymns. I haven't heard hymns for a long time and now I am hearing them, the familiar tunes coming up the hill and this preacher swinging along between crutches.

'I bless the day I lost this leg,' he says, 'for Jesus calls all of us to take up His cross.'

He has seen the way people stare at his missing leg and turns this interest to the Lord's account. He has been called by the Lord to bring the Word of God to this forsaken land. He has known the pretence of human happiness. He has been a soldier in the army of men, drinking and keeping the company of loose women. A cannon-ball took off his leg and he has known the despair of that life that is without Jesus. Now he is a soldier in the army of God. He drinks from the Cup of the Lord and he is in the company of Saints.

'Do they speak English?' he asks me.

I am unable to say because I cannot speak for fear and wonder.

'Cat got it, brother? I was told that this was an English-speaking colony. Runaways are they? I do some speaking in

140

tongues, when the Holy Spirit comes upon me. He knows their language. He knows the words in all our hearts. Helps when they speak a bit of English, though, in the Lord's work.'

In truth, the use of English has declined, except between the Black Cook and Dido; the Black Cook and Hanno; the Black Cook and me; me and Alice; me and Mary; and, most encouragingly, Mary and Alice. A language is developing for communication between the different peoples, and it includes the occasional English word that I recognize by its sound sometimes before I realize its meaning. The Dans use quite a few, believing them to come from the language of the ancestors and the saviour, for whom they carry their sticks in readiness.

'Some,' I manage, but Josiah Peabody has already been surrounded by the Dans, who prostrate themselves on the ground before him.

Josiah Peabody picks up a couple of the carved sticks, gladly offered up by their owners. He breaks the end off one and then binds them together to make a cross. He plants it in the earth.

'The Cross. God,' he points at the sky, 'sent his only son, Jesus, to die for all of us,' he opens his arms to include all of those present, 'on the Cross. We are all of us washed in the Blood of Jesus.'

'Hallelujah,' say the Indians, who have been silent until this point.

Alice approaches with little Elizabeth in her arms. She is followed by Mary, who carries Henry. Mary stands behind me, but Alice goes forward to examine the evangelist Peabody. She spits at his feet and then kicks the prostrate body of the nearest Dan. She breaks out in a torrent of dismissive African. Cutting it off, she turns to me and smiles:

'Wrong leg. Ha!'

Peabody seems confused by this. He follows Alice with

his eyes as she walks away again. The Dans are confused also.

'I bless the day I lost this leg in Jesus' name,' he begins again.

'Praise the Lord!' say the Indians, sensing the moment.

'The Lord created them with fine buttocks,' Peabody confides, still caught in their sway as Alice moves up the hill, 'perhaps in compensation. The Lord's work is infinite in its mystery.'

The Dans are talking amongst themselves, urgently, and Hanno has arrived.

'Welcome to New Carthage.'

'Thank you, sir,' says Peabody. 'Have you heard of Jesus?'

'I have heard his name,' says Hanno.

'The sound of His name is sweet,' says Peabody.

'Yes, indeed,' says Hanno with an ingratiating inclination of the head.

We climb the hill in a procession of sorts. I am walking on one side of the preacher and Hanno is on the other. One of the Indians has plucked the cross from the ground and is holding it aloft. We stop when Peabody sees the ship, in the glory of all its decoration, on the top of the hill, moored, as if on the crest of a wave.

'The ship!' he exclaims.

'Yes,' I answer him. 'It brought us here.'

'I've heard of such miracles, but until this day, the Lord has not opened my eyes to witness one. He lifted you out of the waters. He blows on the mighty ocean and His breath becomes a great hurricano, but in the terror of that storm, you are still held in His gentle hands. He places you on the mountain top and not a hair is harmed on your head. With His little finger, He could destroy us all, but such is His love for us poor sinners, that He lifts us from the eye of the hurricano. Praise the Lord!'

'Hallelujah!' chime the Indians.

142

'We . . .' but I allow my words to peter out. Hanno is saying nothing. What advantage can he see in silence and should I be able to see it? 'Praise the Lord,' I say to the echoing response of the Indians.

'She will make a fine church. A cathedral of the forest,' Peabody breathes in wonder.

'It is the citadel. She is a palace. Scipio Africanus.' I find it hard to explain.

'Strange name for a white man, brother.'

'I am William Bone. Scipio Africanus is . . .'

I think about how I should best describe the events that have led us here and how best to describe the Black Cook, but he has appeared on deck with Dido and they are looking down on us as we approach.

'Scipio Africanus,' I point and Peabody claps me on the back as he gives his crutches to one of the Indians. He hoists himself up the ladder, using the strength of his arms to haul as he lifts his foot on to each rung. I take the crutches off the Indian and follow him. I am followed by Hanno, who carries the plain stick of his office. The Indians, who remain below, begin to sing hymns again.

'Isn't that a glorious sound, Mr Africanus? Jesus has saved them from their godless ways. He has healed the savage breast.'

Peabody smiles into the impassive figure as he climbs over the gunwales. He takes the crutches from under my arm as I appear behind him and swings forward until he is face to face. He holds out his hand in greeting, but the Black Cook doesn't take it.

'The Lord has placed this ship on the top of a mountain as a sign, brother. It is His promise. It is the Ark on Mount Ararat. From here we will conquer the rediscovered world, as the waters of godlessness recede. Do you speak English? This shall be His church in the good fight against the heathen and against the great Anti-Christ in Rome, whose

143

priests are like a sea serpent coiled about the neck of this drowning continent.'

The Black Cook does not answer, but Dido speaks:

'We pull this ship with our own hand, rope on our own shoulder, our own feet against the earth. This is New Carthage. Old gods do not live here.'

'Nothing is old in Jesus, sister.' Peabody keeps his eyes focused on the good eye of the Black Cook, as he addresses Dido. 'I bless the day I lost my leg in His name. Cannon-ball took it off and I gave the rest of me to Jesus, rejoicing in my suffering. I am born again in the blood of the Lamb. He has made me a child again so I may enter the Kingdom of Heaven. I see the beauty in His creation through the eyes of a child. Nothing is old in Jesus, sister. In Him we are made new each day.'

Dido is about to make a reply, but the Black Cook holds up his hand. Where is his cleaver? In my mind I can see him bring it down through the skull of Josiah Peabody, but I don't see the blood. Neither his nor the lamb's. I see the cleaver in the skull of the sailor, where it is momentarily wedged while I wrestle with the arm of his companion. I am tasting a blood madness and I see the cleaver come down a second time. We are here on the same deck and, looking through Josiah Peabody, I see the two sailors. Josiah Peabody stands where Half-Done Dan stands. Their legs complement each other. I would hold their arms for a third stroke but there is no cleaver.

'The ship is mine,' the Black Cook says into Dido's silence.

'We'll carve a great door in the side of her and make some steps leading up to her and we'll fashion a church inside where the cargo used to sit. We'll make a great cross out of her masts and it will be a great beacon of light. She will be seen for miles. Talked of as a wonder. Thus shall the savages of this continent be brought to the glory of God, praise be, Mr Africanus.'

144

'How is it you have come to New Carthage, Mr . . . ?'

'Peabody. Josiah Peabody. I bless the day a cannon-ball took off my leg in Jesus' name.'

'So you have said.' The Black Cook is calm. He speaks in his own voice today.

'He heard stories. He thinks it's a colony of runaways.' Am I trying to make him angry? Do I recognize in him now, the instrument of our fall? I am afraid. Hanno is still smiling. I hate him, because his calculations are so finely made.

'Is this true?'

'The Lord sent me from the island of V—, where I was doing His work amongst the good Christian souls who have made of that place a garden with their plantations. The Lord smiles upon the island of V—, but He wanted to test me. I shall test you, Josiah Peabody, in your body and in your soul, said the Lord. Test me Lord, saith Josiah Peabody. Your work shall be among the heathens of the continent, not on this island of righteous ways. I took a passage to the colony at W—, which is a foothold of our countrymen on this mainland, north of here and a hard, testing journey of the soul through the wildernesses of God's creation. I made Christians out of the Indians, who were abject savages before they knew the Lord, and I built a church with their hands. It has flourished in the sight of the Lord, like unto one of those rich plantations in the warmth of the sun, it has ripened. But again, I heard the voice of my Lord: I would test you, Josiah Peabody, in your body and your soul. Test me Lord, saith Josiah Peabody. He has tested me, but I bless His name for I have come through. I was told by my Indians of this colony of English-speaking runaways and Indians and white men and a ship that the Lord has placed on a mountain and I said to myself: Josiah Peabody, the Lord is calling you to this work. You must be about His business. This ship is His church, cast upon a mountain top

145

as a beacon from which the light of the Lord shall shine forth across this continent. I recognized His voice, you see, and I said to myself: Josiah Peabody, you are like unto that ship, yourself, for you have been tossed back and forth on the oceans of the world. A cannon-ball took off your leg in Jesus' name like a raging hurricano, but the Lord has plucked you from the perilous sea where you would surely have foundered and He has placed you on the Rock of Faith, which is like a mountain. This is a sign, Josiah Peabody. Well, I went down on my knee, because the Lord in His love left me one knee so that I might pray, and I prayed. I prayed and the Lord sent me to Major Tulliver, who commands the garrison at Fort X—. Take them the Lord's word, Josiah Peabody, said Major Tulliver, for he is a good Christian and he raised the money for this expedition amongst the plantation owners. My needs are not great, said Josiah Peabody, for the Lord will provide. I took ten of my best Indians and we have made this journey. Are the ways of the Lord a test for the honest pilgrim?'

'Major Tulliver?' asks the Black Cook. I am listening, because, as he lifts his voice into this question, he is also telling me for the first time that story of Major James Tulliver and Mrs Tulliver and Master James and Miss Lucy and in my imagination I see him as he describes himself, that little Roman in his bright new costume.

'He is blessed in the sight of the Lord.'

'Is he an old man?'

'He has passed the half-way mark of his allotted span, but no, he is a man of middle years like you or I.'

The Black Cook says nothing more on the subject, but he radiates a sense of pleasure. It is the first happiness I have seen in him for so long. I am glad of it and I dread its implications.

'So word of our fair city has spread along the coast, the subject of travellers' tales.' He does not wait for an answer,

146

but continues: 'You may take protection within the walls of the city, rest, eat and travel on.'

'This is the place', says Peabody, 'God has called me to.'

'Our crops have not been good this year, but we have many furs and we have the skins of many crocodiles. What goods have you brought with you?'

'Nothing but the Name of Jesus,' says Peabody.

'I have matters to consider. William Bone, here, will see to your lodgings.'

Dido is frowning deeply at Josiah Peabody, but says nothing. The Black Cook smiles at Josiah Peabody and indicates that the interview is at an end. He turns and Dido follows. I lead the evangelist down the ladder to the waiting crowd, where his servants are already hard at work with the various Indians of our number, spreading salvation.

'Hallelujah!' says Josiah Peabody and the Indians from their various conversations turn and answer him.

Hanno puts his arm around me. It is difficult for him to do this, but he keeps his smile. He asks confidentially: 'Do you know this Jesus?'

'Of him,' I tell Hanno. 'I know of him.'

'Is this good or bad?'

I cannot answer him. My small kingdom, such as it is, finds protection within the city walls which I now see crumbling before they have been built. The whitewashed plasterwork cracks, sending fissures running across the surface like roads through fields of wheat. The evangelist Josiah Peabody and his Indian servants carry a great cross with which they are battering down the walls of New Carthage, a collection of rough huts scattered across a hillside in the lee of a beached ship. The kingdom of love has no protection. Josiah Peabody and his Indians are singing a hymn. I can hear myself joining in because I know the words and I am in need of comfort. Hanno is trying to join in, watching my lips and guessing each word as it comes.

147

Where he thinks he has got it, his voice is suddenly all confidence. The next phrase and all his confidence is gone, but then it is back. We are singing and it is his voice that I can hear most clearly.

Major James Tulliver, what sweet destiny brought you to these shores? Were you carried on the breath of Jesus over the stormy sea? How is your sister? And where are you now?

TWENTY-TWO

Tonight I am lying awake in this shelter with Alice and Mary. Our two children are asleep. Alice and Mary are asleep. I want to wake them up. Pokey-pokey. If I had the strength for a hundred times apiece I would do it now. Wake them up and do it. I want to see myself doing it, but I want to watch them in their sleep also. I am watching them in their sleep, because I do not wake them up. There is not enough here. The kingdom is too small. It rises and falls too quickly. I want to hold their bodies. I want to see myself holding them. Instead, I see myself lying awake holding on to nothing. The kingdom is filled with nothing and with moments of love that cannot be held.

The evangelist Josiah Peabody does not leave. He has erected a tent on the flat lands below the hill among the failed crops. His Indian servants have carried his tent on their backs from the colony at W—. I am watching them erect it. Josiah Peabody does not erect it, but rather orders its erection. He sits on a rock and blesses the day a cannon-ball took off his leg in Jesus' name while a large cross is fitted together from a couple of straight poles cut to receive each other and then bolted. Although there is no shortage of wood, here in the forest, the Indians have carried this with them also from the colony at W—. They have brought their own spades and they are digging a hole, into which

149

they will plant the cross, some ten feet in front of the tent. They are gathering small rocks with which they will wedge it upright. They are filling in the hole.

The Dans have started bringing offerings of food to the visitors, who have brought their own cooking utensils and have laid out their own fires a little way away from the Temporary Church of Our Lord Jesus in the So-Called Colony of New Carthage, near to where the Indians have made their own shelters. They have made new sticks for themselves, plain and shining smooth, with a small cross-piece at the top. Peabody is greatly heartened by this demonstration of their faith. He does not understand it, but knows it for the work of God, who has reached into the savage breast and claimed it for His own. In the thin soil of these failed croplands, he tells the story of Jesus in pictures with a stick. Today he is telling them the Miracle of the Feeding of the Five Thousand. He is drawing many people in the dirt. He looks up into the faces of the inquisitive Dans and points to each of them. He points to New Carthage as if to say: 'More.' He says: 'Five thousand.' They nod and repeat the words after him. Now he is drawing Jesus, who has a halo on his head and stands in front of a cross. He lets them know that he is playing Jesus. He points to the picture and then to himself. He beckons a small child from the picture and takes an imaginary parcel from his hands. He holds up three biscuits he has brought with him from the colony at W—. He holds up five fish caught this morning in the river, and cooked specially for the sermon. He breaks the biscuits into crumbs and gives the crumbs out. He throws the remaining fragments to the five thousand who are gathered behind the Dans. He breaks up the fish and gives each of the Dans a tasty morsel, throwing the heads and the tails behind them to the crowds they turn to see but do not see. 'Five thousand,' he repeats. 'Five thousand,' they repeat. 'That's Jesus for you,' says Josiah Peabody in

150

triumph. 'Jesus,' say the Dans. They nod in wonder as the evangelist cannot eat any more, his stomach swollen with providence. He slaps it contentedly and they slap theirs.

They are a celibate order, the Dans. They eschew women after the manner of their saviour. Women might open their legs, but a Dan's eyes are on the horizon, watching for the saviour's return. In the general shortage of women, here, no one opens their legs to the Dans, whose celibacy is a convenience. It is another sign of the Lord's work to Josiah Peabody. They will slide into Christianity very easily, as the doctrinal work progresses. They have abandoned Alice, upon whose singsong stories they used to hang like bees around a honeypot.

Alice taps her head: 'Stupid Dans. Foolish mans. Like these stories not understand. Not enough pokey-pokey, William Bone.'

Mary is attracted to the pictures in the dirt: 'You know Jesus?'

I tell her: 'Yes.'

'Like Two-World Dan?' she asks.

'No,' I tell her.

'Not like Two-World Dan,' she says.

'Wrong leg,' says Alice.

'Jesus has two legs,' I say in an attempt at explanation, which I abandon.

The Indians who came to New Carthage before have now moved down to join the Indians who came with Josiah Peabody. The Africans whose Indian women have moved out, have followed them down. Half of New Carthage now inhabits these flat croplands. The preacher welcomes all who will live in Jesus.

I am welcomed as a fellow Englishman, but I am berated as a bigamous sinner.

'I see you writhe in Hell in a torment of flames. Oh you writhe in the pleasures of the flesh, now, between your

151

two harlots, but each instant of pleasure shall become a thousand tongues of fire in the next world. The grinning demons who shall be the scourge of your eternal suffering will have the black faces of your bastard children and they shall laugh over you as you beg for forgiveness but it will be too late on that sulphurous day. See your harlots curse you for their own suffering as you shall curse them. Come to Jesus, William Bone. Abandon the ways of fornication and come to Jesus. He is waiting for you. He weeps over your sinful life. He will welcome you into His bosom, William Bone, but you must walk down the hillside alone. The breasts of women shall not save thee. The lips of women whisper in your ears, yes, on the left and on the right, but their words shall not save thee. The scented fingers of women move across your body, aye, from the left and from the right, but they shall not save thee from the fiery pit. It is a primrose path, between their legs, but it leads to the very gates of Hell. Turn back, William Bone. Even now you can hear the sweet sound of Jesus' voice. He's not whispering. He is crying out so that you might hear Him. His voice is a mighty wind that can quell those flames or fan them into fury: Turn around! Come to me, William Bone! My servant Josiah Peabody has need of you!'

Mary's eyes are wide open as she listens to the rise and fall of his voice; to the sweet pleadings; to the mighty wind. But he doesn't always talk to me like this. Sometimes he puts his arm round my back. He has to put both crutches in his other hand for this manoeuvre. He leans on me for support, the stump of his thigh hanging between us.

'Together, William Bone. You will help me and I will help you to Jesus.'

He has his eye fixed upon the ship, his great cathedral. Looking up towards her from the Temporary Church of Our Lord Jesus in midst of the wreckage of our attempts at crops, he sees the Black Cook looking down and it is as if Josiah Peabody is the Captain of the Lord's Host, laying siege there. She will be a mighty prize. He covets her for Jesus, to whom she will be worth more than a thousand savage souls, for she is a vision, vouchsafed to him by the Lord.

With his eye on the ship, he is filled with love for me, because Jesus has made me the instrument through which everything shall be achieved, sinner though I am. When I see the cross of Jesus raised above her decks, I cannot help but see the error of my ways. Perhaps I will take Mary and make an honest wife of her. He has watched her. She has not set her heart against the Lord. In marriage, even the gates of Hell may be consecrated to the Lord's work. But he has seen the Devil at work in Alice's eyes and he must wrestle with the Devil, wherever the Devil appears. If he must wrestle with Alice, he must wrestle with her. The Lord tests him in his body and in his soul. But it is I who must persuade this Africanus to deliver up Josiah Peabody's cathedral of the forest.

I can see the ship in his eyes. He has been caught in the Black Cook's vision, although he does not realize it. This ship is just a ship. An elephant is just an elephant. On top of this hillside, however, it is something more than itself. Decorated with the flowers of the forest, some like scarlet stars, some a deep blue; there are rich oranges and yellows against the leaves and branches that seem to grow out of the timber with which she has been constructed; she is more than something more than itself, she is her own story. This is Dido's work, continually renewing the flowers and the foliage. The Black Cook's work has fused with Dido's work and this is what Josiah Peabody sees, with his eyes wide open like Mary's, listening to the Black Cook's Story, which he cannot understand, but he marvels at it. I can see this. He is afraid of the ship in the same way that he fears the Lord and he loves the ship in the same way that he loves

153

Jesus. He would gather up his host and storm her, but he wouldn't harm her. This is why I am the instrument of Jesus' will, through which everything is to be achieved. I know this. I can see it in his eyes, although he doesn't speak to me of it. I see his eyes following Alice for a moment, the sway of her fine buttocks as she returns from the forest, a dead animal slung over her shoulder and various fruits gathered in her cloth.

'We should pray, William. Kneel with me.'

I kneel with him, because, after all, he is a fellow countryman, even though I am afraid of what he brings in his eyes.

Tonight I am telling the Black Cook all of this, but he isn't listening to me. He is lost in his voices again. I have given up listening to his voices. He has become remote.

'You must fight him,' I say.

He signals that our interview is at an end, but I lead him by the hand and point over the side of the ship. He has become gentle in his movements and doesn't resist me.

'Do you see that? The Temporary Church of Our Lord Jesus? It is Rome. You can strike now. You can destroy Rome. What has happened to you?'

'That is not Rome,' he says. It is his own voice again. 'It is a tent. Someone has built a cross in front of it. It is the preacher.'

'He is dangerous,' I say, but the Black Cook has walked away from me.

It is as if the Black Cook, rising to this height above the world, has emptied himself. He sits on top of this vessel and beneath him, the vacuum of his absence sucks in another emperor and another empire. This is how the world can survive, for if emperors held on to the space beneath them, there would be no room between a thousand empires for a man to move. We would be crushed between their straining borders. The same must be true of the kingdom of love. If

154

it wasn't for this emptiness, love itself would crush all love out of the world.

I can see this now. I have lost the kingdom beneath me. This is merely absence filled with ghosts, but ghosts have no substance. I am writing about this emptiness and absence so that the door will burst open under the pressure of it and the new kingdom shall come.

Yes.

I will have to stand on the table or I shall be knocked down by the force of it.

No.

Because I have no substance. The rats do not speak to me any more because they don't recognize ghosts, who have no meat at all. They will live in the next kingdom as they lived in mine, oblivious to these things.

TWENTY-THREE

It is evening and I have come to him again. He is walking the deck in the company of his voices. He has become his own historian, improvising on a text by Livy. He does not need me. He does not pay attention to me.

THE BLACK COOK IMAGINES A MEETING

The two greatest soldiers of the age: the equal to any king or general the world has ever seen. Their admiration of each other closes their mouths. They gaze on each other in silence.

Africanus speaks:

'So many times has Victory been almost within this grasp, if Fate has decreed this now, at least she gives me you and not another from whom to sue for peace. Is there not a sweet irony in the weave of Fate? I took up this struggle when it was your father who was Major James Tulliver, and now I come unarmed before his son. If the gods had given our fathers happiness with their own continents, yours with Europe, ours with Africa, it would have been for the best. What is done is done. It may be censured but not altered.

'We did attempt to gain that which did not belong to us. Now we fight in defence of our own. You have seen

156

the enemy almost at your gate, just as in Carthage, we now hear the noise of Roman tents. Major James Tulliver, you approach these discussions from a position of strength. This brings you happiness. It brings us none at all. Your government and my people will agree to our decisions in this field. You and I have most to gain from a peaceful settlement. In our negotiations let us keep an even temper.'

Do we see Major James Tulliver the Younger nod his assent? Africanus continues:

'I am an old man. I left my homeland as a boy. The great weight of success and failure that has been my life teaches me that now I should follow the laws laid down by Reason, not hope for some stroke of luck. You are young . . .'

Here, the Black Cook pauses for a while, suddenly confused. He sees Major James Tulliver as a boy. The laws laid down by Reason tell him that he is not a boy. He sees himself as a boy before the battles of Trasimene and Cannae and he sees the boy Tulliver knock him to the ground again, for this is his place. Anger crosses his face and disappears in a calm sea.

'A man's heart may well prefer the chance of Victory to the possibilities of Peace. I have a better understanding of the aspirations of the soul than of the political mind. Did fortune such as yours once smile on me?'

Here, he pauses again. He looks up through the richly decorated rigging of his ship. The sun is shining and the flowers hang like victory flags.

'The greater the success of a man's enterprise, the less must we trust it to endure. The sun shines on the hour of your ascendancy. For us, all has become dark.'

157

He gets up and strolls about the deck arguing with himself, but now he stops short.

Major James Tulliver replies after the following manner . . .

The voice like salt:

'I am aware of human frailty; neither do I ignore mighty Fortune. All we do is at the whim of a thousand chances. It seems most improbable that I am here at all, does it not, and yet I announce myself. I am under no obligation to take account of your feelings, am I? Did I ever take account of your feelings?'

'You are not,' admits Africanus, 'and you never did.'

'Do you offer us compensation for the ship which you took; for the cargo that you took; for the violence against our envoys?'

'I do not,' says Africanus. 'Look about you . . .'

The Black Cook looks about him, through his own eye; through the eye of Africanus/Hannibal; through the eye he has allotted to Major James Tulliver.

'Do you see anything of value?'

'I do not,' says Major James Tulliver.

'I can offer you nothing, then,' says Africanus.

'It is evident that you find Peace to be intolerable,' says Major James Tulliver.

'I do,' admits Africanus.

The Black Cook turns to where Dido is waiting with his cloak and three-cornered hat. There is no place for me here. He goes back to his galley. I am climbing down the ladder that hangs over the side of the ship. It is as if I have missed

158

something that has been said to me. The sound of it reverberates in my ears, but I can no longer hear the words that were spoken. Even though everything is now in the present and the words are still being spoken and I can watch them being spoken as I watch myself climbing down the ladder, I see myself continually missing the words. His mouth is moving like the mouth of a fish. I am on the ladder and words rise through the air.

TWENTY-FOUR

The Dans are gathered about the door to our hovel. Mary is among them. She has brought them there. She peers, like them, through the door at something that is occurring inside. A miracle, perhaps.

The silence with which they have approached our door contrasts sharply with the eruption of their voices as they witness this thing. This explosion of noise, in turn, leads to the loud voice of Josiah Peabody. It is the clarion sound of denunciation.

'I can see you, Satan!'

The Dans and Mary see, rather, Josiah Peabody trying to pull up his breeches in a hurry, against which intent, the absence of one leg is a disadvantage and so he is still struggling as I reach the doorway myself. The Dans clear a path for me.

'I was wrestling with the Devil.'

Alice is propping herself up on her elbows. She is laughing.

'I have been wrestling for your eternal soul, William Bone.'

Alice is putting the cloth skirt around her waist. She looks at me without shame. She looks at me with triumph. Mary looks at me with embarrassment, but she also wants to laugh. Alice is speaking to the Dans.

160

'She is the Devil, that one,' says Josiah Peabody. 'We must cast her from our midst. The Lord has created her breasts to give delight to a man's eyes, but Satan has turned her milk to bitter gall. The Lord has created the softness of her black skin, but Satan has made her heart like stone. We must cast her from our midst and and she will sink like that stone through the deep waters of the river. She shall sink even unto Hell itself. I have wrestled with this Devil and I know her now.'

'One-World Peabody,' says Alice. She wrenches the crutches from his grasp and he goes down in the dirt.

'I bless the day a cannon-ball took off my leg in Jesus' name for the Lord is testing me.' He is biting his lip as he says this. He is crawling away from Alice, because she is lifting the crutches in her hands. She is striking him as he crawls through the dust. She is spitting on him.

'Test me, Lord, in my body and my soul!' cries Josiah Peabody as the blows rain down upon him, but now Alice is turning her attention to the Dans. She is attacking them with the crutches, driving them away. She is screaming at them and now she suddenly stops and throws the crutches at their false saviour, who is lifting himself from the ground on one of the Dans' abandoned sticks.

I do not know what to say. Mary puts her arm round me. She does not know what to say either. Our kingdom is falling about me, but Alice is in a wild mood. Her face close to mine, I am looking in her eyes to see if I too can see the Devil, but the Devil is in my eye. We have tried to live in this kingdom. This is her way of trying to protect it. I can see this. She does not understand history. I want to tell her that I understand history. She doesn't understand me.

'Not enough pokey-pokey. I give him. Good, yes? Everybody see him arse up down. Ha! Yes? William Bone happy family.'

161

Her hands are against my ribs now.

'Yes,' I say. I can see her hanging from the rafters.

'Good,' says Alice and she slaps my hips. She turns and goes back into the shelter. She is bringing me my fiddle. 'Music,' she says. 'Play jig for Mary. Her eyes open for you, yes? Better than Jesus Peabody. Yes.'

I am a cuckold for my own good. I can see this. If I could only see only this. In my imagination I see Jesus Peabody's arse going up and down, wrestling with the Devil, his one knee scratching about for a purchase in the bed of soft grasses and leaves, his stump not knowing what to do in the struggle with his enemy. I cannot see his eyes but I know that they burn with righteous lust. His hands grasp Alice's shoulders. He wants to take hold of her breasts, but even in his zeal he knows that he will topple over unless he has a firm grasp of something, so he grasps tightly on the shoulder diagonally opposite to his good leg and feels with his other hand, but he feels himself going so he presses his chest down against her, trapping his free hand so that he has to pull it free anyway. Alice is laughing, but he does not see this, because his mind is occupied with the difficulties of his position. He puts his hands against the soft grasses and levers himself up, inclining his head strangely so that he can get his mouth around her nipple. It is then that he hears the commotion in the doorway; tastes the bitter gall where milk and honey ought to flow; feels this heart of stone; sees his adversary for the first time.

She has the Devil in her eyes. I have a different devil in mine. I have never been counted among the saved. Jesus Peabody is an invading army. The borders of my kingdom have been violated. I am playing jigs for Mary and Alice and Henry and Elizabeth, but my heart is somewhere else. I am looking around the walls of this hut and everywhere I see incursions. Mary is holding Henry's hands as he sits in her lap and she is clapping them together. She is smiling hard at me because she wants me to be happy, but she knows I am not happy.

He is being lured into an ambush so that his army can be destroyed. I can see this as I imagine his arse going up and down. I see Alice coming from the forest or maybe she is coming from the river. There are fish outside the door. She is coming from the river and she sees the zeal in Jesus Peabody's eyes. She whispers something to Mary, who is walking down the hillside to greet her. Henry and Elizabeth are playing in the fine earth.

'Bring me to Jesus, yes?' she is asking him and he is swinging on his crutches behind her. His tongue touches the inside edge of his lips and he imagines it in the marks of the scourge across her back. He is thinking of the scourge with which they drove Our Lord upon the hill of Calvary. His eyes are on the sway of her buttocks. They are telling him a story as he swings along to their rhythm.

Now I see his arse going up and down. I can still see it. I can always see it, the hairs and pimples of it. Up and down as the bow across the fiddle. It has no story of its own. Alice is laughing because she has ambushed the armies of Jesus. I am not laughing because she has ambushed merely the vanguard of a much greater host. Mary finds no magic in my music. She wants me to laugh so that the music might improve. Outside, there is a shot.

The Black Cook is standing on the hillside in his cloak and three-cornered hat. He has a pistol in his hand which has been discharged into the air. New Carthage is gathering around him, such of it that remains on this hillside. Hanno is there. He carries a musket now, having dispensed with the staff of his office. He knows whose side he is on. Dido is there and she carries a pair of pistols.

'Listen!' cries Hanno, looking to the Black Cook for approval momentarily before he translates his own word.

'His tents are gathered in the fields of wheat, which he

163

has destroyed in the tramplings of his feet.' The Black Cook delivers each line so that it might be translated and Hanno translates it with an unusual terseness, so that I suspect simplification. 'He has laid siege to the city, for he envies its might and covets its wealth. He had no part in its building, which you undertook with the strength of your own hands. He will take all this from you.' He casts his eye around his city, encouraging the Carthaginians to do likewise with the gestures of his hands. 'The glory of victory is more attractive than the slow starvation of waiting for defeat. See, I have brought muskets and swords. If you know how to use a musket take a musket. If you do not, take a sword. If there are not enough swords, take up your own sticks. Let the gates be opened. Let us drive him from our land.'

Those that gather round him now have no love for Josiah Peabody, who threatens them with fire because they do not walk down the hillside to make their shelters there. They are happy that the Black Cook is back amongst them. He is the only one to whom they owe a particular debt of gratitude. They cheer. They make the noises of war in their throats and we are coming down the hillside. The evangelist has gathered his Indians about the Temporary Church of Our Lord Jesus. They are singing hymns. They have muskets in their arms too.

The Dans are sitting apart. They are at the edge of the forest, gathered to themselves, and want no part in this.

I have a pistol in my hand.

'Give me the ship,' says Josiah Peabody. The Indians are not now singing.

'You are not in a position to make terms.'

'Mr Africanus, the Lord has given me that ship. I am the instrument of His will. He has placed that ship here. It is part of His plan that I should wrest it from you. His will,

164

Mr Africanus. Do not cross the Lord for He is mighty in His wrath.'

'Leave these lands. They do not belong to you.' The Black Cook is calm.

'He spoke to me. He showed me this place in a dream. These lands belong to the Lord. He has sent His servant to claim them.' Josiah Peabody is not calm. 'Sitting in your pride, you are the king of this country, Mr Africanus. Oh yes, King Africanus, mighty Emperor Africanus, but kings and emperors, what do they add up to? They are insects before the glory of God. They crawl about the Earth like beetles on a dung heap. You are nought but a black beetle, Mr Africanus. In the Lord's good time, He shall crush you under His foot. Give me the ship, for the Lord has created beauty and I must create a cathedral: a beacon of light in the darkness of this continent. See, the breath of life is being squeezed from her by the coiled serpent of Roman popery. With our sword shall we smite the serpent. Cut it in two, so that the halves wriggle helpless in the dust. We shall build a city for the Saints, gleaming white in the protection of the Lord. Can you see it, Mr Africanus?'

I am levelling my pistol at his forehead.

The Indians are raising their muskets and Josiah Peabody is sheltered behind them.

'William Bone, if I did anything to you it was the Lord's will. His will. The Devil is at large in this continent and he must be driven from it. I'll drive him!'

'You may leave the city. You may take the clothes you are wearing. You will leave unarmed. You may take the memories of your wives and children.'

Faced with a certainty he cannot begin to understand, Josiah Peabody is already edging backwards awkwardly, between his crutches, towards the river. The Black Cook does not disarm the Indians, who, contrary to his instructions, are busy gathering their belongings. He raises his arm

165

and lets it fall. The Carthaginian host moves across the land.

'Leave the cross,' says Peabody. 'It shall be a sign that this is yet God's country.' God's purposes combine desire and pragmatism in His servant Josiah Peabody. 'Most assuredly He shall claim it.'

If the Lord is a military strategist, His servant is not. As a soldier in the army of the Lord, he has chosen his ground badly. He is retreating. His Indians and some of the converts form a defensive shield to protect both him and themselves as the flanks of the Black Cook's forces open to the left and the right. The two armies stand facing each other. Victory smiles in the faces of the Carthaginians and their opponents have been defeated in their souls already.

Josiah Peabody turns from his retreat in this moment of eerie silence. He is not a military strategist but he is enough of one to recognize a hopeless cause. He turns again and hurries away. His body swings between the crutches. The arse bobbing back and forth, back and forth over the rough ruins of our agriculture. He has trampled our fields of golden wheat. Up and down. I raise my pistol again and fire. I am aiming at this arse, but I miss and hit one of the Indians, who falls to the ground. The shield breaks and they are all running. The retreat has become a rout. All around me, the Carthaginians are raising their weapons and letting fly at these figures running towards the river, carrying their evangelist with them.

The Black Cook is walking back up the hillside. He sees the laurels of victory. He doesn't care to see his army now running wild through the camp of the Temporary Church of Our Lord Jesus, taking vengeance on converts whose faith is not strong enough to make them leave with the preacher, but now they too are running down towards the river and some of them are falling and dying in the gullies of this pitiful landscape, their blood flowing down towards the

166

river still, where Josiah Peabody has now reached the other side.

I am standing over the body of the Indian I brought down and I am listening to his groans. They are mixed with the cries of those who are being beaten or hacked to death. So few, because most of them ran into the forest and because, anyway, we are few and now we are less, but I have this body groaning at my feet and I am not looking at the carnage of this field, but at his arse that rises and falls with his groans as he tries to accommodate the pain that cannot be accommodated. I lift a rock from the earth and crush his head.

Tonight I am alone. I can hear myself singing:

> 'Who is that jolly butcher boy?
>   His name is William Bone.
> Pray, why does a jolly butcher boy
> Live by himself alone?
>   Well, why shouldn't he?
>   Oh, why shouldn't he?
>   He don't need a wife
>   If he's quick with a knife
>   And all the ladies have gone.
>   Fa la! Fa la!
>   Fa titty fa la!
>   Pray, where have the ladies all gone?'

They are gone. They do not like this murderous strand in my personality, but we are not responsible for what we inherit. I was born in a butcher's shop. That was my country. Do they see themselves hanging from the rafters of my smoking shed? No. I am not my father. I have the wrist movements but they are movements of love. I make no pies. I have no ovens, and, besides, jelly does not keep in this climate. They do not understand me. I am trying to

167

make them understand me, but Alice has closed herself to words that can be understood. She has a rock in her hand and, see, she crushes my fiddle across the bridge. Mary is holding Henry and Elizabeth and they are crying. Mary is crying. Alice is an hurricano. I am the still centre around which she whirls. She has me in her hands. She abandons me on a mountain top like a ship bereft of the sea. She is gone. I am trying to hold on at least to Mary, who is crying, and to Elizabeth and Henry, but the wind is too strong.

The Dans are afraid. They are reappearing at the edge of the forest in ones and twos. They are looking over the battlefield, where the dead lie unburied in the rain that falls in thick sheets from the sky. In their shelters, the Carthaginians are drinking and sharing out the Indian women who are now their slaves. The rain could wash it all away and into the river, but it doesn't. Alice is leading the Dans back into the forest. Mary and Henry and Elizabeth go with her. My children, who do not resemble me at all, are walking through the paths of the forest, with their different mothers, beneath trees I will never climb. They are walking and they are carried, for they are still small, but they are gone.

I am imagining the collapse of the kingdom and this is not it, as I imagine it, but it is, nevertheless. Night and the rain and I am stumbling across the flat lands amongst the corpses. I am drunk and I am still drinking from a gourd I have been given. The rain splashes on the surface of the wine, which spills over the edge of the gourd. I don't know if I am drinking the rain or the wine. Both bring their own kinds of oblivion. I find no comfort in the Indian women and that is why I am here, searching for the fragments of love before they are washed down through these gullies that catch my feet.

I can hear myself singing, but I am not singing as loud as the rain, which sings so very loud, as it runs across my face as I lie in the mud next to a body I do not recognize. I am part of the rain, for it has soaked through all of my clothes and I am running down towards the river. I am washed in the rain. It is forgiveness like the aftermath of an hurricano.

I am all that is left.

TWENTY-FIVE

Here in my cell, today, I see myself writing this history. This is not the first attempt. It is like crossing the Alps: there are many routes, but not all of them will accommodate elephants.

The first time, I write this history for you, Major James Tulliver. I write it to free myself from prison, but you never come. The gaolers do not speak to me. You are an old man, perhaps. Maybe you are dead.

'These are curious events, William Bone,' you are saying. 'This was Scipio Africanus, given to us by our father?'

'Him,' I say. My eyes are hollowed out with hunger and I cannot say much.

'Our little general,' says a woman, indignant at the thought, and I realize that this must be Lucy Tulliver, although I don't know what she is doing here at Fort X—, on the shores of this hostile continent. She must have her own story. I cannot read it in the movements of her body, because she wears too many clothes.

'Same,' I say. I am unable to stand.

'And Scipio Africanus taught you to read and write, so that you might be his historian?'

I nod.

'He was always too clever for his own good,' thinks Major James Tulliver.

'He used to carve me little dolls out of pegs,' says his sister, for this is the hardest thing to understand.

'Write this history for me, Bone.'

I see you telling me to write. I see myself writing, but I do not see you any more.

The second time I write it, I am writing it for the Black Cook. I write to find a freedom from history, which has claimed and populated each flagstone on the floor of this cell so that I cannot walk from my bed to my table to the shithole without negotiating ghosts.

'Write it down,' says the Black Cook. He is standing in chains and I am standing in chains. Hanging is too good for him, so he is flogged and his tongue is drawn across a block and chopped off, so that he will lead no other rebellions, and they pull his bollocks across the same block and castrate him so he will spawn no further rebels. Dido, also, they flog and they remove her tongue. And the others. They are separated into lots and shipped to different colonies, people with no story to tell.

I write for you, but you are gone and even Major James Tulliver talks of you as if you are a dead thing, although you are alive, maybe, an old man on a plantation that is blessed in the sight of the Lord, or maybe you too are dead.

The third time, I write it for Mary the pig-keeper's daughter and Mary the mother of my son, Henry, and Alice, the hurricano, mother of my daughter Elizabeth. I am writing to be free from responsibility and from the sweet taste of them, the scraps of them in their own jelly.

'Not good,' says the hurricano, lifting a stone and crushing my fiddle, and I am watching, unable to say or do anything to stop it, because the hurricano does not understand that it has been sucked into an emptiness.

How can emptiness be responsible for anything? If it isn't responsible, how can it ever be free from responsibility? And can you fill pies with air?

171

The fourth time I am writing, I am writing to be rid of it, to be free from meaning. I am writing down each incident so that it is finished with. If I had my fiddle, I would play every tune I ever learnt or composed, so that I could be rid of them, too. I am writing for the rats, who talk to me and now don't talk to me, because, for them, I am already not here. They wait for the next prisoner who will replace me, now that I am dead, not completely dead, but enough dead.

I do not visit the Black Cook now. He is in his palace with his queen. She no longer tends to the rigging. The flowers are wilted and the leaves are turned brown. Their story continues, but I do not know it.

The Indians shun us now. Our Indians slip away in the night. They are walking through the forest in search of new cities. Perhaps they will find Alice, who is building a city somewhere. Mary's eyes are wide open as, brick by brick, it rises in her hands and Henry's hands and Elizabeth's hands and the Dan' hands and they are no longer a celibate order. Alice is laughing, building a singsong city in the tops of the trees. She is untroubled by the marks of whips. She lies on her back on the broad platform she has built in the trees. Her city rises above her. Let us call it Y—. Children fall out of her like fruits hanging from the branches. Her laughter is louder than the rain, which is louder than my tears. In Y—, there are no kings or emperors. There is no Scipio Africanus, no William Bone, no Jesus, no Dan, who is drowned at last. Her stories are of the forest and this world.

We survive on this hillside. Already it is covered in new growth that nobody clears. I do not eat. I eat sometimes. I am tossed a fish sometimes. I ask for nothing, except palm wine. We know we are waiting for the end.

See, Major James Tulliver, I am writing the end, now. Will you come, now that it is the end? I hear no footsteps.

Your ship will sail into the mouth of the river R—. Hanno will see you. He will walk through the flatlands and down to the river and greet you. There will be fire in the eyes of Josiah Peabody, who will be on your right hand in this day of judgement, and Hanno will hang from the yardarm, his legs kicking and struggling and then still, because there is no negotiating with Jesus. The Black Cook will not see this, but I will see this. Some of the Carthaginians will see this and they will take up arms, but they will lay them down before the redcoated marines.

The Black Cook will see them at the foot of the hill, marching up the rough road. He will surrender. He will stand in chains on the hillside.

The evangelist Josiah Peabody will claim this beached ship for Jesus, for a cathedral of the forest. He will enter it. He will leave his crutches behind, because he cannot climb the ladder and hold them at the same time. He will steady himself on the rigging and on the gunwales, hopping across the deck. He will enter the cargo hold. He will lower himself down into the depths among the slave stalls. In his imagination he will measure it for Jesus, its vaults and pews. The Black Cook will not see this, for he has forgotten it all. You, Major James Tulliver, you will not see this, for you are busy rounding up runaways. I will see it.

I will hear you command your marines to gather brushwood and build a fire beneath this ship on the top of a hill in the middle of the forest, because you have not seen Josiah Peabody climbing up the ladder in a frenzy of zealous lust, in the vanguard of the Empire of Jesus. You will command your marines to light this fire, however, because you are a general and you serve a different empire. Jesus is merely in

173

your sphere of influence. You will never understand this ship, but you will know that it must be forgotten.

I will see the ship burning. Josiah Peabody will burn in the depths of his cathedral and the gold-edged pages of Livy's History of Rome will burn also.

I will see the broad avenues of white-painted houses, burning.

I will feel the strong wind, blowing through the flames.

TWENTY-SIX

I am imprisoned on the island of Z—. Here, there is no wind. I have written this to free myself from silence. I am writing about flames I no longer see. I will climb the steps to the door of my cell. Crouching like a small child about to be beaten by his father, I will cover my head with my hands. Behind me I have created such emptiness that the door will burst open and the winds will rush in. The door will pass through me, because I have no substance. I will walk through the corridors of this prison until I find daylight.